FOR THIS MOMENT

The Gentrys of Paradise

HOLLY BUSH

Holly Bush Books

For Helen

CHAPTER 1

May 1871 Paradise, Winchester, Virginia

"ENCHANTED," RICHARD ARMSWORTH SAID AS HE BOWED LOW.
Olivia Gentry watched him, interested to see if he would kiss her hand. He seemed content with rubbing his thumb softly on the back of it while touching the pulse of her wrist with his fingers. It was intimate, and unsettling as well.

"It is a pleasure to meet you," she said.

"Miss Olivia is the secretary for the Young Women's Society here in Winchester," Mayor Fitzhugh said and turned to her. "Mr. Armsworth works for Governor Walker."

Olivia smiled at the mayor's introduction and glanced up at Armsworth. With not a sidelong glance to Fitzhugh, he was staring at her in an intense fashion, making it seem as though he was unaware of anyone else in the ballroom at Paradise, her family home, that evening. She turned to the mayor, drawing her hand from Armsworth's as she did, and purposefully looked at the older man.

"Are you enjoying yourself, Mayor Fitzhugh?"

"Oh yes! There are always fine foods and spirits served at Paradise, and the ballroom looks like you've brought the garden inside!"

"Why, thank you! Mother and I and Aunt Brigid thoroughly enjoyed decorating for tonight's party, and the gardens cooperated even though it is quite early in the year."

Fitzhugh turned as he heard his name mentioned. "Ah. There's Reverend Pendleton. I must speak to him."

Olivia looked at her new acquaintance. "What brings you to Winchester, Mr. Armsworth?"

Armsworth considered her, his clear blue eyes focused on her face. He tilted his head and smiled, his mouth full of even white teeth. "I would say 'you,' except we've not met before this evening, and even with this very brief acquaintance, I don't imagine you appreciate a man dissembling."

"I do not," she said and looked away from him to survey the room. *My oh my.* Her heart was beating rapidly. Richard Armsworth was a handsome man and perhaps dangerous. He was still looking at her when she turned back to him, and it seemed he'd stepped closer to her, crowding her, although the distance he stood from her was surely the same as it was before.

"I've heard of you, though, and aptly described, too."

"Heard of me? I doubt that, sir."

"I'm a guest of my aunt's, combining business with some pleasure," he said.

"Your aunt? She lives here in Winchester?"

"She does. Moved here from London not too long ago."

"Mrs. Barrett? The lady who built a large home a few miles from the western edge of town?"

"Yes. Dear Aunt Agatha. She was Lady Monticue in London but preferred not to use her title once she arrived. She likes to think of herself as a 'commoner' now that she's come to America. Thinks she'll fit in better with her new neighbors," Armsworth said with a wry smile. "Of course, my aunt Agatha would never be mistaken for anything but exactly what she is."

Olivia chuckled and then looked chagrined. "Oh, dear. I'm so sorry. I shouldn't have laughed. I've met your aunt. I would never mistake her for anything but exactly what she is, either."

He laughed aloud, revealing fine lines around his eyes. He was handsome when serious and devastatingly attractive when laughing. His hair was gold blond, thick, and trimmed to perfection. He was broad-shouldered and long-limbed and had an easy masculinity.

"She wrote me about you, you know."

"About *me?*"

He nodded and smiled charmingly. "She was very adamant that I meet you. She described you as very beautiful and lively, and bright and well-spoken, although she is concerned that you're growing a bit long in the tooth."

"Long in the tooth?" Olivia said, laughing. "I *am* old compared to my friends who are already married with one or two children. My mother has told me that when the right man comes along, I'll know right away. I don't believe I've met the right one yet, though!"

He took her hand in his and stepped closer to her. She could smell his cologne and feel his body heat. The laughter in his eyes had been replaced with something akin to pleading.

"It is my wish to change your mind on that subject."

"Oh," she said and swallowed. "How clever you are. I didn't mean to beg for a compliment."

"I'm sure you didn't."

Olivia couldn't seem to drag her eyes away from him, and she felt the heat of a blush rise from her chest to her face.

"Am I interrupting something?"

Olivia turned, her cheeks warm, to her brother Matt. She stepped back quickly. "Of course not. Have you met Mr. Armsworth?"

"I haven't," Matt said with a smile, extending his hand. "What brings you to Winchester and within six inches of my sister, Mr. Armsworth?"

"Matthew!" she said.

"My apologies, Miss Gentry, if I have offended you or your family," Armsworth said smoothly, with a nod to Matt.

She watched as Matt pulled Jim Somerset forward to join the conversation. She'd known Jim since she was a small girl. He and Matt were the same age and had been friends all their lives, having met as young boys when Jim's father, the local farrier, serviced the Paradise horses. She'd long been over her girlish dreams of him from the time when his patience with a friend's younger sister had made him her champion.

"Armsworth? Jim Somerset is an old friend of the family," Matt said and looked at Jim. "Mr. Armsworth is going to tell me all about his work for the governor while you dance with Olivia."

Matt turned toward Armsworth, giving Olivia his back and leaving her facing Jim. He was staring at her with his typical unreadable look.

"I suppose I can hardly blame you for your part in Matt's scheme. More than likely he dragged you over here, away from the punch bowl and the food, on some shaky pretense so that he could—"

"Armsworth was standing too close. Your brother had an obligation to see to your welfare."

"I'm well old enough to see to my own welfare."

"Stories about Mr. Dunderage have been repeated to him. He's your brother. What do you expect him to do?"

Olivia's hands shook, and she was unsure if she was going to scream out in anger or cry. "Will my mistakes made as a young girl haunt me forever? Do you believe me so shallow that I was unable to learn any lessons? Am I such a child in your eyes? Get out of my way," she said bitterly and began to step past him.

He didn't move. "You should dance with me. You're very upset, and I'm sorry to be the cause of it."

"Why would I want to dance with you?"

"Because you don't want to speak to anyone else at this party when you're this angry."

She looked away over the crowd in the ballroom. Guests everywhere were laughing, enjoying meats, cheeses, dainty sweets, glasses of wine or punch, reacquainting themselves with neighbors after a cold winter with few social events. He was right, even though it was hard to admit. She didn't want to speak to anyone right now. She looked up at him, and he winged his arm, leading her onto the dance floor.

The musicians began a waltz, and she placed her hand on Jim's shoulder as his hand went around her waist. Her skin tingled where he touched her through her pale green satin gown. She looked up at him, at his humorless face, his dark hair, longer than she thought necessary, the thick beard that covered his cheeks and neck, and his plain white shirt, stiff with starch and stretched tight across his chest and arms. He was as comfortable as her oldest riding boots and not quite as interesting.

But that wasn't fair. She knew he was well-read and intelligent. Knew that he was a town leader and had been responsible for his mother and younger sisters and brother since his father's death years ago. And even though his face was humorless, he was an attractive man, and a favorite of many of the unmarried women in town and a few of the married ones, too. She'd stopped thinking about him as being handsome or attractive years ago, though, when she'd been fifteen years old and he'd told her he wasn't interested in her and never would be. It had shattered her virginal heart into a thousand pieces.

Olivia watched the other dancers as they went by and was content to let her anger fade away as he twirled her around the dance floor. She turned her eyes back to his face, and every surety she had of her own indifference to Jim Somerset fled as if she'd pulled on those comfortable boots and run away, past the stables and into the woods.

His eyes were not focused on her face but rather on the low neckline of her gown. Her mother had been concerned about that neckline, but Aunt Brigid had told her she was being a goose and that a young woman as beautiful and shapely as their Olivia should always don a gown so flattering.

Jim slowly raised his eyes to hers. His face was flushed, and even with the music and conversations flowing around them, she could hear his short breaths. But it was his eyes that made her swallow and her hand tremble on the rigid muscles of his arm. He'd been staring at her bosom now rising and falling, at her cleavage, she was certain. He twirled her faster around the edge of the room, spinning her without missing a step or bumping into the slow movers, and staring at her all the while, his eyes hooded and dark and intense. She was unable to break his gaze, trying desperately to keep up with his rapid double-time steps and the staccato rhythm he set. His hand at her waist tightened, and she felt a shot of aching restlessness from her breasts to below her waist. The waltz was familiar, but this dance was not.

The music ended and he stopped suddenly, sending her against him from breast to knee and caught in his grip on her arms. He set her away from him firmly, and none too gently.

She dropped her arms to her sides, feeling awkward and uncomfortable. Her mother and Annie, her sister-in-law, were staring at her from just a few feet away, Annie's mouth agape, her mother's look calm and steady. Jim went away hurriedly, leaving her alone as the dance floor began to fill again. She was not certain she trusted her legs to carry her.

"My oh my," Annie said and took her hand to lead her off the dance floor and to her mother's side. "What good dancers you are."

JIM SOMERSET LIT A SHORT CIGAR AND WANDERED DOWN THE stone drive of the Paradise ranch. He could hear the music through the open windows of the ballroom, still lit up brightly when he took a sidelong glance over his shoulder. It would be a shame to ask his mother and sister to leave this early, but he wasn't sure he could go back in the ballroom and face her. Olivia Gentry, that was. He wondered if there was any amount of distance he could put between them to get rid of the awful tension he felt.

She haunted him. Wafted through his dreams like a specter. Shortened his breath when he saw her at a distance and gut punched him when she was close enough to touch, as she was tonight. He took a long drag and dropped the cigar, tamping it out with his boot. He'd cured himself of her, hadn't he? Long ago he'd decided he best find himself a nice woman to settle down with and have some children. They'd learn to be a comfort to each other as they grew older. But every time he met a woman for dinner or danced with one at a social, thinking he'd best begin courting, he found himself unenthused. Blasé enough to not be tempted to steal a kiss. What would a lifetime be like with a woman he didn't want in that way? One that didn't stir his blood. He could learn to appreciate her sewing or her cooking or her child-rearing skills, he imagined. Would it be enough?

Somerset wandered back toward the house, past the front doors and open windows of the ballroom, hearing snippets of conversation as he went, to the stone terrace at the back. He settled on a wooden bench and listened to the night sounds from the close forest of trees. It was cool and the hum of the party faded to the background. He consciously listened to the hoot of an owl, the chirp of crickets, and the yowls of barn cats set to fight each other.

"Oh, I'm sorry," Marabelle Winston said as she stepped out of the house.

Jim stood as she approached. "No need for an apology. We can both enjoy the night air."

He watched her shoulders rise and fall and then she walked to him and sat down on the bench. He sat down beside her. Her hands were folded neatly in her lap and she was staring straight ahead. He'd known her for quite a few years and saw her often working in the mercantile for her father. He was never a man for small talk but Marabelle was clearly nervous or upset and he thought he best try and put her at ease. Surprisingly, she began to speak before he could remark on the temperate weather.

"Your mother told me that you'd gone outside. I came out to look for you."

He turned to her. "Oh? What is it, Marabelle?"

But Marabelle didn't say another word. Instead, she latched her lips to his, leaning in and laying a hand on his chest. He did move, nor did he have any inclination to move. In fact, he sat very still for what seemed like minutes, although it was likely only seconds. Her eyes were closed. His were not. Out of the corner of his eye, he saw someone pass behind the window in the Paradise kitchens that looked directly on to the terrace. He hoped he and Marabelle were in shadow, as he wouldn't want her to be the subject of gossip and didn't want to raise any expectations among his family, or hers.

But then he thought perhaps Marabelle would be someone who would be a good wife and mother. In fact, he knew both to be true. She was kind and loyal and hardworking. She was quiet, although apparently not as shy as he'd thought before. The problem remained, however, that he was mentally evaluating her, with no desire to move this kiss beyond touching lips. He waited until she sat back, and he could see that she was breathing hard. Even in the shadows, he could see her blush.

"I am not beautiful, but I enjoy your company and hold you and your family in high regard. There. I've said it."

"Thank you."

Her head turned sharply to him. "Thank you? What do you mean by that?"

"You said you hold me in high regard. I was thanking you for it."

Marabelle's shoulders dropped, and he heard her sigh. "It is a lovely evening, but I'm chilled now. I'll be going in. I'm sorry to have bothered you."

"It was no bother."

She stood and turned to look at him. "I'll never be her. No one else will."

He watched her retreating figure and heard the door close as she went back into the house. He really was not good at whatever he should be good at where it concerned women. Clearly, Marabelle was hoping for a declaration of some kind. *I liked kissing you. I loved kissing you. I want to kiss you more. I hold you in high regard as well. You're beautiful.*

But it would have all been a lie had he said any of it. Marabelle was a pretty young lady but not beautiful, not to him anyway. Surely there would be a man who thought she was the most beautiful woman in the world. That was not him. But what had she meant when she said, "I'll never be her. No one will"?

CHAPTER 2

Olivia lolled about in bed the morning after the party. The rain that had thankfully held off the day before was coming down gently now. The window was open an inch or two and she could hear the patter of the drops as they hit the overhang below her window and Jenny, the Paradise housekeeper, shooing Red, the family dog, out the kitchen door. It had been light out for an hour, or maybe more, but it seemed as though all the Paradise residents had slept in a bit after the party. Then her door opened with a bang.

"Livie," Matt said from the doorway. "Can you help Annie with Teddy while she gets dressed. I'm going to hitch the team."

"Maybe knock the next time you barge into my bedroom, Matthew," she said as she stood and pulled on her robe. "Have some respect for my privacy and person."

"You're my sister," he said and walked over to her dressing table. He picked up a pot of rouge and smelled it. "What is this stuff? Why do you wear it?"

"Get out of here, Matt. I've got to get dressed if I'm going to help Annie."

"What's the matter with you this morning?"

"There's a man in my bedroom picking up my things and sticking his big nose in them."

He smiled crookedly, and she was reminded why women fell at his feet. Her brother was ruggedly handsome and annoyingly male. Annie seemed to be the only person, other than their mother, who had any semblance of control over him.

"I don't have a big nose."

"Go!" she said. "Hitch the team."

She dressed hurriedly, pulled back her hair with a ribbon, and knocked on Matt's bedroom door where he and Annie stayed when they visited Paradise overnight.

"Come in!"

"I'm here to hold my favorite nephew while his mother takes a moment for herself," she said and picked Teddy up from where he was trying to crawl to the edge of the bed. "Give me kisses, little man," she said and nuzzled the child's face. He responded by giggling and pelting her with baby fists.

"I've got to use my tooth powder and pull up my hair. Won't be more than a few minutes," Annie said and stepped behind the screen in her room.

"Don't hurry," Olivia said. "Teddy and I are just fine. Do you still need me to come help you with the garden?"

"That would make the planting go quicker, if you have time."

"The party is over, so I've got plenty of time."

Annie's head popped out from behind the screen as she brushed her hair. "The party was wonderful! I felt like I was in a fairy story. All the food and flowers, even with summer not yet here."

Olivia sat down on the bed watching Teddy examining his toes. "It was wonderful."

"You don't sound like you thought it was wonderful at all!"

Olivia shrugged. "I was furious with Matt for what he said in front of Mr. Armsworth. But otherwise, I suppose . . ."

"He told me what he said," Annie said as she came out from

behind the screen and pulled on a blouse over her chemise. "Sometimes he hasn't the reasoning the Lord gave him, and I told him that. Who is this Dunderage person that he and Jim were talking about?"

"Timothy Dunderage. I was almost sixteen and he was eighteen and not from a very nice family I found out much later. I was leaving for schooling shortly after he told me he loved me and wanted to marry me," Olivia said with a little shrug. "I wasn't seriously considering it but was flattered with his attention. At the church festival that summer we walked hand-in-hand to the stables, supposedly to see his new horse. There was no one inside as everyone who worked there and even Mr. Wilkins was at the festival. I suspected nothing, of course, even though I wondered why he kept looking over his shoulder to the barn doors. He kissed me passionately and had his hand on my chest when my father and his walked in on us."

Annie's hand came to her mouth. "He wanted to be caught, do you think?"

She nodded. "He did. He and his father thought that the Gentrys would make very nice wealthy relatives. They were sharecropping on a run-down farm outside of town and were hoping to purchase it."

"Do you still see him at church and such?"

"They moved on shortly after that," she looked up and said. "I was mortified. My father saw me in a heated kiss with a man's hand on my breast. I didn't leave my room for weeks."

"And then Matt says what he did."

"I was embarrassed in front of Mr. Armsworth."

"Of course, you were! He is a handsome man, if you hadn't noticed."

"I noticed."

Annie chuckled and then sat down on the bed and waited until Olivia looked up. "What is between you and Jim Somerset?"

Olivia shook her head and looked back at Teddy. "Nothing. Nothing at all."

"Oh. It seemed as though there might have been some history between the two of you after he danced with you, staring at you like you were an apple dumpling, just waiting to eat you up, and then leaving the party."

"He didn't leave. His mother and his sister Nettie were still here, and I'm sure he took them home. And anyway, I saw him on the terrace with Marabelle Winston. He was still here, just outside getting some air, I suppose."

"After that dance with you, he would have needed to cool off."

"I don't know about that."

"Tell me about Mr. Armsworth," Annie said as she pulled Teddy's night shirt over his head and wiped him clean with a warm cloth.

Olivia repeated what she'd learned about him. "And we're to be at a meeting of the Ladies Hospital Aid and Recovery next Tuesday at the home of his aunt, Mrs. Barrett. So, I will see him again, I imagine, unless he is doing work for the governor, that is."

"Work for the governor. My oh my, how far I have come," Annie said with a smile. "The only fellows I knew a few years ago were the ones who took my pigs to slaughter!"

Olivia laughed, too, and thought about what she would wear to Mrs. Barrett's.

* * *

"YES, MOTHER," JIM SOMERSET SAID, "MARABELLE FOUND ME."

He was sitting at his desk in the room he used as an office behind Somerset Farriers. There was a bed there, too, that he'd been sleeping in more often than not, rather than in his room at his mother's house next door. At twenty-six, he was too old not to have some lodgings of his own and felt ridiculous when his mother treated him like he was still a child instead of a man grown. But he said nothing to her to indicate he was looking for a house or a cabin of his own, even though he'd made a few inquiries. She had never fully recovered from the death of her husband, he felt, and was now oddly fragile where she'd always been steady.

"Well, that's nice," Louise Somerset said and glanced at him. "Did she have anything of interest to say?"

"No."

"She's a lovely young woman, I think, and I also think she's going to make someone a good wife."

"I'm sure she will."

After some long minutes, Louise rose and went to the door. "Breakfast is ready."

"Thank you."

"Morning, Mrs. Somerset," David Freeman said as he held the door and tipped his hat.

"Good morning, David. Please tell my son that it is high time he took a wife."

"Yes, ma'am."

The two men stared at each other for a few moments as Mrs. Somerset left the office. Freeman was Jim's sole employee, gladly retained after Jim's father died and the family business came to him. Jim had learned how to work the forge, trim hooves, and settle an anxious horse from Freeman, perhaps even more than he'd learned from his father, who'd often been out talking to new customers.

"Don't say it, David."

"Say what?"

"Whatever it is you're thinking about that's making you smile at my expense."

"She's right, you know."

Jim closed his ledger account book on his desk. "And you're an expert on this subject?"

Freeman chuckled. "Well, I am married and that makes me

more of an expert than you, that's for certain. Your mother was married, too."

"She was," Jim said and sat back in his chair, thinking about his mother and father. They weren't chatty or overtly affectionate with each other, and he didn't think he could ever remember his father kissing her publicly more than once, and that had been a peck on the cheek; but he'd never doubted that they loved each other. Was that a child's wish or some innate knowledge that family members were privy to? His mother still grieved to this day, with his father being dead nigh on eight years now. Maybe what his mother wanted for him wasn't always on the face of things.

David cleared his throat. "The schedule?"

"What?" Jim asked and dropped the front two legs of his chair down to the floor.

"Today's schedule. I asked you for the schedule."

"Oh. Light day," he said and picked up his calendar book. "We should be done by noon. Let's plan on fixing the back corner of the forge shed later today."

"Yes, sir. I'll get started."

"Here's your breakfast," his sister Emmaline said as she opened the door. "Good morning, David. Have you eaten?"

"Yes, I have, Miss Emmaline. Thank you. I'll just be getting started on the shoes for the McIntyres," David said and went out the door.

Emmaline plopped the plate down on Jim's desk and sat down on his bed. "Eat, so I can take your dirty dish inside."

Jim picked up the fork she had handed him and ate the eggs and ham and buttered bread on his plate. Emmaline lay back on his bed and closed her eyes.

"Why didn't you go to the party at Paradise last night, Emmaline?"

"Didn't want to."

"Why?"

"You didn't want to go. You went because you thought Matt Gentry might be mad if you didn't."

"I went because our mother wanted to go and Nettie needed an escort with John out of town."

"But you didn't want to go."

"I've cleaned my plate," he said and pushed back from his desk. "Thank you for bringing it."

"So, did Marabelle work up enough courage to kiss you?"

"What? Where did you hear that?" he said as he stood. "Tell me, Emmaline. Tell me right now."

His sister opened her eyes and looked at him. "No need to shout. You don't scare me, Jim. I overheard Nettie and Marabelle talking. You know she's loved you forever."

"What are you talking about? Loved who?"

"Marabelle. She's loved you forever. When we were young and Marabelle would come over and she and Nettie would embroider together; they used to let me sit with them. We always had to sit in the kitchen on the hard chairs because Marabelle didn't want to miss seeing you and you would never come in the sitting room where the soft chairs were."

"I didn't know."

Emmaline sat up and shrugged. "I know. Nettie told her she thought she should just get you alone and kiss you. Marabelle has been in a panic ever since that day from what Nettie has told me."

"Why would Nettie do that? Why would she say that?"

"She thinks you need a nudge, and she's happy with John so she thinks everyone should be married."

Jim looked closely at Emmaline. She could never compete with Nettie for beauty, but she was very pretty in her own way, and full of wit and fun. She dressed rather drably, not that he knew that much about ladies' clothes, but he had four sisters and always thought that Emmaline hid behind her brown dresses and gray wool skirts. "Has Nettie been after you, too?"

"Nettie can fuss as much as she wants. It has little effect on me, and I'm guessing Marabelle's kiss had little effect on you."

Emmaline was staring at him waiting to hear his reply.

"I will not besmirch a lady's reputation," he said.

"As I thought." She stood, picked up his plate, and marched out the door.

CHAPTER 3

"It's just the two of us for the Ladies Hospital Aid and Recovery meeting, Olivia. Aunt Brigid is sniffling and wants to stay indoors and pamper herself. Ben will keep her company with the checkerboard. And I've yet to convince Annie to join," Eleanor Gentry said to her daughter in the dining room at Paradise Tuesday morning.

"Will you want the buggy hitched?" Olivia's oldest brother Adam asked as he helped his mother be seated.

"Maybe we could ride, Mother," Olivia said. "What do you think?"

"I haven't been out for a gallop for weeks with the preparations for the ball. Yes. Let's ride. Adam, will you have Silky saddled for me?"

He looked at Olivia. "And who will you be riding?"

Olivia blew out a breath and put her elbow on the table. "With Paint sold, I don't know. Who do you suggest?"

"How about Golden? She's a bit taller than Paint but she's got an easy gait and lots of spirit. I think you'll like her."

"She sounds fine, Adam. A work saddle please."

Her mother looked at her. "You intend to wear a split skirt to Mrs. Barrett's?"

"I do."

"Do I sense an argument? I'll be happy to eat in the kitchen with Mabel," Adam said with a smile.

"There's no need for that, Adam. I understand that times and mores change. Olivia is an accomplished horsewoman and also a lady. Anyone who implies otherwise is mistaken."

"Is this the same Olivia who used to climb trees and throw walnuts at her brothers?" he asked and laughed.

"I am no longer a child, brother," she said. "And perhaps you should share that with Matthew."

"What has Matt done now?"

"He embarrassed me in front of Mr. Armsworth and then gossiped about me to Jim Somerset. I did not appreciate it at all." she refilled her cup. "More coffee, Mother?"

"No, thank you," Eleanor said. "What did Matthew say that was so upsetting?"

Olivia told the story from the night of the ball. "I knew my face was bright red when he said it. Mr. Armsworth was crowding me a bit, and I was just stepping away."

Adam shook his head. "Matt and Jim have been thick since they were eight years old. I wouldn't call it gossip. There is likely little that they don't share, and certainly Matt was watching out for you just as I would do or Father would have done."

"You don't understand, Adam," Olivia said sharply. "I'm not a child, and I found it particularly rude that Mr. Somerset brought up a person from my past, my long-ago past, at a party hosted at our home. I would prefer to never see him again." She stood and put her napkin on the table. "I will be ready at ten o'clock, Mother."

Adam and Eleanor watched her leave the dining room in a hurry and heard a door close loudly a short time later.

"She never wants to see Jim Somerset again? Isn't that a bit extreme?" Adam asked.

Eleanor Gentry raised her eyebrows and sipped her remaining coffee.

ELEANOR AND OLIVIA TROTTED OFF DOWN THE GRAVELED PATH that lead to the road into Winchester. Olivia patted Golden's neck. She was a lovely horse, exactly as Adam had said, and the morning was beautiful, too. The air was pleasantly cool, and the new leaves were moving gently in a soft breeze.

"What a perfect morning," Eleanor said as the road brought them to a spectacular view of the valley, with Winchester in the distance. "Your father loved spring."

"I miss Daddy still. I keep thinking that it will go away, that ache I feel every time I think of him, but it does not."

"Beauregard was such a large presence," Eleanor said and looked over her shoulder at Olivia. "I miss him, too. Very much."

"He had a way of sorting things out for me in a simple fashion, and he treated me like an adult. He never treated me like a child."

"We walk a fine line between allowing our children to make decisions and understand consequences, and keeping them safe. When Matthew left home to join the war . . ." Eleanor looked away.

"I had never thought of Matthew's leaving from your point of view, Mother. I was too angry and frightened."

"Your father and I discussed it at length and had some disagreements over it," Eleanor said as she steadied her mount when a rabbit shot out from the undergrowth.

"Disagreements?"

Eleanor nodded. "I wanted your father to go after Matthew and try and reason with him, but he refused. It was for the best, of course. Matthew found Annie and became a man in the whole of it."

"But what if he had died?"

Eleanor closed her eyes. "Is the length of a person's life the measure of it? Or are we destined to do our best in the circumstances the Lord puts in front of us? Although I begged God every night to take me and bring Matthew home safely."

"Perhaps Father was praying the same."

Eleanor glanced over at her. "Perhaps he was and perhaps the Lord answered him."

"We're being gloomy, Mother. I'm wearing my new split skirt and my dress boots. I should be rapturously happy."

"You should be, I agree," Eleanor said with a soft smile. "Let's give these horses their heads for a bit."

Olivia kneed her mount. She leaned close to the neck of the mare and enjoyed the rhythm of the horse's gait and the breeze at her face. She glanced at her mother, who was smiling broadly as she pulled her horse down to a trot. Olivia slowed Golden as well and noticed the mare favoring her right front hoof. She got down and pulled the horse's leg up.

"I don't have a pick with me and she's got a stone under her shoe," she said as she came around the horse to remount. "It's not large, but I think I should get her back to Paradise."

"We're closer to Winchester than we are to home. We'll go directly to Somerset's and he'll take care of it," Eleanor said.

"I'll walk her home."

"And miss the meeting at Mrs. Barrett's? She's barely favoring it, and we're close to town."

Olivia glared up at her mother. But it wasn't her mother's fault that she was angry, and she didn't deserve her short remarks. She mounted and set the mare to a slow walk. "I would prefer not to stop at Somerset's. Perhaps Jasper at the stables will have a pick."

"I'm sure they will have a pick, Olivia," Eleanor said and stared at her steadily. "Is this because you are still angry with Jim?"

"I will be angry with him forever!" She felt tears at the back of her eyes. She turned her head quickly to the landscape.

"Olivia? You seem very upset over a small indiscretion. Jim and his family have been friends of the Gentrys from the time your father and I settled here. I hate to see any continued animosity."

She took a deep breath. "You're right, Mother. You're absolutely right."

JIM WAS CRAWLING AROUND ON THE FLOOR IN THE BACK corner of the forge shed, checking that he had filled all the gaps between the new stones with mud. He tapped a stone a hair or two farther into place with the wooden handle of the trowel and wiped the sweat off his face with his sleeve. He'd need a dunk in a tub or in the creek soon.

"I'll help you in a minute, Mr. Somerset," David said from the open end of the forge. "The McIntyre horses took me longer than I thought."

"I'm fine, David. Just take care of the customers." He was in no mood to talk to anyone if truth be known. He was furious with his sister Nettie, and at the situation with Marabelle. He might as well admit he hadn't slept well for thinking of Olivia Gentry in that shiny green gown she'd worn for the ball, or the feel of her in his hands, or the color of her lips. What a fool he was!

"Miss Olivia? What can I do for you?"

Jim sat back on his haunches when he heard David and the other voice that followed.

"It's my mare, David. She's got a stone in her hoof."

"Let me take a look."

Jim shot to his feet, and there she was getting down from her work saddle in a buckskin-colored split skirt that showed off her curves. His pulse raced. The wise thing was to just keep his filthy, sweaty body out of view, double-check the new stones one more time, and keep his mind firmly on his business. And she was not his business.

"Do you need any help, David?" he asked instead. He picked up a rag and wiped his hands as he walked around the forge and into the late morning sun. "Mrs. Gentry? Can I help you while David looks at the mare?"

"Yes. Thank you, Jim," she said. "Is there a block?"

"Right over here." He held out his hand as she unhooked her leg from the pommel.

"Thank you. We were on our way to the Ladies Hospital Aid and Recovery meeting at Mrs. Barrett's when Olivia realized her mare was favoring her leg."

"Mrs. Barrett's?" Jim asked.

"Mr. Armsworth's aunt, if you remember. I believe you met him at Paradise last week," Olivia said.

"I know who he is," Jim said.

Eleanor glanced at both. "I imagine we'll see your mother and sister at the meeting, too."

"Marabelle Winston will be there as well," Olivia said and brushed her gloved hands over her skirts.

Jim stared at her, and she met his eyes. This was the second time within a week it struck him that he was not good at these parlor games, or any games really. He didn't care for the under-tones and the subterfuge she employed. He was ready for straight talk whether it discomforted her or not. But her eyes, while defi-ant, held another emotion. Pain. Something had hurt her. Or maybe someone had. Had they been alone, he wouldn't have trusted himself near her. As it was, Mrs. Gentry cleared her throat.

David had apparently pulled the stone from Olivia's mare's hoof and was giving a leg up to Mrs. Gentry. He and Olivia continued to look at each other until she turned abruptly and pulled herself into her saddle. She turned the mare without a word and trotted toward the end of town.

"Thank you, David," Mrs. Gentry said. "Please add this to the Paradise account."

Jim looked up at her. "There's no charge." He went back inside the forge and knelt for another look at his uneven stones.

"AH, THE PARADISE LADIES ARE HERE!" MRS. BARRETT SAID AS she stood from her chair near a massive pink marble fireplace. "We were becoming concerned, weren't we, ladies?"

"We're so sorry to keep you waiting," Eleanor said as she smiled, moved forward, and took Mrs. Barrett's outstretched hands in hers. "We decided to ride today instead of bringing the buggy, and Olivia's horse picked up a stone." She turned to Mrs. Somerset. "Fortunately, we were able to make it to our local farrier's without issue but it did delay us a few moments. Your Jim and David took care of everything."

There were fifteen or so women in the room, Olivia noticed, all in some of their best daytime finery. Her tan wool split skirt was among the latest fashions she'd seen when she and her mother and Aunt Brigid had taken a trip to Philadelphia early in the spring. They'd brought pictures back for Bessie, the woman who'd bought Aunt Brigid's seamstress shop, and bolts and bolts of fabric and lace and buttons. But she knew that no one in the town of Winchester was quite ready for her ensemble. Bessie had made her a short collarless jacket to match in black and tan plaid with just the thinnest thread of red. Her split skirt hung above her ankles and showed off her low-heeled buff dress boots.

Sarah Englebright stood and clasped Olivia's hands, her eyes shining. "Olivia! What a beautiful outfit. This is a split skirt for riding, is it not? I am mortally jealous as I am wearing this ridiculous bustle that does not allow me to even sit correctly!"

Olivia laughed. "I have never been fond of sidesaddles. Or bustles!"

She looked around the room, determined to forget the tension she'd felt ever since seeing Jim Somerset. How could a man as filthy and sweat-covered as he was make her insides quake and focus every one of her scattered thoughts on her breasts and the private area between her legs? The muscles in his arms had rippled in the glare of the sun and were dusted with dark hairs. There was nothing slender about him, and Olivia was used to big men. Her father and Adam were tall and well-muscled, and Matthew was larger yet and powerful-looking. She was not short herself, yet the top of her head barely reached Jim Somerset's shoulder. His chest was nearly as deep as his shoulders were wide and there was not an ounce of wasted flesh or fat on his person. His dark hair and thick beard only added to her impression of him. He was a giant and capable of making her thoughts flit away in the wind.

"Did you bring this style back from Philadelphia?" Sarah asked.

"Are you sure our little town of Winchester is ready for such . . . forward styles?" Mrs. Barrett asked.

Eleanor replied, a gracious smile on her face, "Our business, our *family* business, is horses. Olivia has a stake in that business and is a progressive-thinking young woman. She'll be poised with her brothers to continue the horse breeding business or another business venture if she chooses. However, she is a lady first and foremost. I think she looks very pretty."

All eyes turned to Mrs. Barrett, who raised her brows and narrowed her mouth. There was a long moment of silence. "I will have to agree then, Mrs. Gentry. Horses are her family business. Why shouldn't she be a leader in the fashions associated with elegant women who are also exceptional riders?"

"Exactly," Eleanor said.

Olivia watched her mother greet the rest of the older women, while she turned to Nettie Winders and Emmaline Somerset, Jim's sisters, and Marabelle Winston.

"Well," Olivia said, "I have passed muster with Mrs. Barrett it seems."

"I was waiting there for a moment to see if she would have you bodily removed," Nettie said and giggled.

"What horse rot," Emmaline said. "Who cares one bit what you're wearing."

Marabelle looked longingly at Olivia. "I would never have the courage," she said in a near whisper, "but it is so beautiful."

Olivia smiled at Marabelle. "Your dress is lovely! The color is perfect for you, and I do like the flower-printed silk for the collar and cuffs."

"Mother insisted. I was going to ask Bessie to use plain fabric, but Mother thought I could use a bit of 'livening up.'"

The door to the sitting room opened and a formally dressed butler announced that luncheon was served. They all removed to the massive dining room and were seated. After their meal, they began their meeting in the library, where chairs had been set up in a large circle. Mrs. Barrett and Eleanor Gentry had a small table in front of them, covered with notes and papers.

The door opened and Richard Armsworth came inside. Olivia was certain she could hear the collective patter of female hearts as he did so. She watched him as he kissed his aunt's hand, made a bow to her mother, and begged their forgiveness for his interruption. He spoke with nearly every woman there, recalling some small detail of their meeting or a past conversation, as if he'd memorized every circumstance. He was charming without being obsequious, good-humored without being silly, and confident without any trace of conceit. Add in his physique and blond good looks, Olivia thought to herself, and one would declare him to be the perfect man. Why then, did he not have much appeal to her other than to look at, much like a beautiful painting or vase?

His eyes and smile found her at that moment. He made his way around the circle of chairs and spoke to her directly.

"Miss Olivia. You are looking particularly fetching today. I see this style worn by the most fashionable ladies at our state capital."

"Thank you, Mr. Armsworth," she said, feeling the eyes of every woman in the room on her.

"I'm organizing a picnic here at my aunt's home, in two weeks," he said, continuing to stare at Olivia. "Please all consider yourselves and your families invited. We'll have a casual meal out of doors and some games for the children and some dancing under the stars, too."

"How lovely!"

"I will be looking forward to it!"

"It will be the talk of Winchester for those two weeks!"

Armsworth broke the connection between the two of them and looked around the room with a broad smile. "I hope you will all come and be prepared to be entertained."

Olivia smiled, too. How could she not? Everyone was talking about what they would wear and marveling at Mr. Armsworth and Mrs. Barrett's generosity. Laughing with Dorinda Blevins when she declared she might get a chance yet to dance with Mr. Delgado, the new schoolmaster.

"Perhaps Miss Gentry would honor me with the first dance of the evening," Armsworth said into the now silent room as he returned his eyes to hers.

Olivia could hear sighing behind her as she stared up at him. He had maneuvered her neatly. She would look petty if she denied him in front of these women, yet her affirmation would take root as the beginnings of a courtship. Good manners required a response regardless.

"Why, thank you, yes. I would be delighted."

Armsworth left the room after kissing his aunt's cheek again and exacting promises that everyone would come to the picnic. As if anyone would miss it! The door closed and Mrs. Barrett finally had to call for quiet to resume the meeting. Olivia barely heard a word as the women discussed their plans to purchase a piece of land for a hospital from the money they'd been raising over the years.

While everyone gathered their wraps and carriages were being brought to the front of the house, Nettie, Emmaline, and Marabelle pulled Olivia to a corner.

"He is so handsome!" Nettie declared. "If I wasn't mad about my John, I'd say he's the handsomest man I've ever seen."

"Don't be ridiculous. He's handsome, but so is John and Matthew and Adam and Jim and Mr. Delgado," Emmaline said to her sister.

Marabelle licked her lips and whispered, "But he does have a certain sophisticated flair, don't you think?"

They looked at Olivia expectantly. She shrugged. "He is very handsome."

"That's all you can say? I just keep thinking of him without any clothes on," Nettie said and slapped a hand over her mouth. She looked at Emmaline. "Do *not* tell Mother I said that."

* * *

"PASS THE PEAS TO YOUR BROTHER," LOUISE SOMERSET SAID TO her youngest daughter, Jane.

"I don't want peas," Phillip said. "I hate peas."

"Mind your manners, Phillip. Say 'no thank you,'" Jim said as he sliced a piece of roast beef on his plate. He sat at his father's place and had taken on the settling of some typical family squabbles, especially those disagreements that began with Phillip, the youngest in the family and doted on by his mother and sisters, other than Emmaline, of course, who doted on no one.

"No thank you, Jane," Phillip said, smiling innocently.

"You should eat your vegetables, Phillip," Louise said. "They're good for your digestion."

"Cook said there is cherry pie for dessert. Aren't cherries vegetables?"

"No, they are not," Emmaline said and put a few peas on her brother's plate. "Eat them or I will stuff them up your nose."

"Emmaline!" Louise said as she laid her fork and knife down. "Please. Have some manners at the dining room table."

"How was your meeting today, Mother?" Betsy, the middle child and often the peacemaker, asked.

"It went very well! Mrs. Barrett's home is lovely, and the luncheon was delicious! Real china, I tell you, she served us on real china. It was Wedgwood, every dish and plate matching for eighteen of us! I always counted myself lucky that I had four plates that weren't chipped." Louise shook her head.

Betsy smiled. "It sounds lovely! I wish I was old enough to go!"

"Oh, but there is more exciting news," Louise said and looked directly at her.

"More exciting than the china?" Emmaline asked dryly.

Louise glared at her but turned back to Betsy with a broad smile. "You may not attend a meeting just yet but there is to be a picnic hosted at Mrs. Barrett's home by her nephew, Mr. Armsworth. We are all invited! There is to be a meal, games for the youngsters, and music, too!"

Jim looked around the table. Betsy, Jane, and Phillip were asking questions of their mother excitedly. He'd likely be required to escort his mother to the paragon's picnic or his sisters and brothers would never speak to him again.

"Wasn't it interesting that Mr. Armsworth asked Olivia Gentry to dance the first dance with him at the picnic. Such an honor for her," Emmaline said and sipped her lemonade, staring straight ahead.

Jim growled. He couldn't help himself, and it wasn't an under-his-breath sort of noise of dissatisfaction but rather a loud grunt. Settling the first dance with Olivia was just the kind of thing a man like Armsworth would do. Many would think they were courting. Perhaps they were.

"Jim!" his mother admonished. "Excuse yourself. Yes, Betsy

and Jane, you may leave the table to begin working on your dresses for the fete! Phillip," she began, but as soon as Phillip heard his name he was out of his seat, banging open the door to the kitchen. "That boy. What shall I do with him?"

"Apply some discipline, Mother," Emmaline said.

"I'm going to get a hat to wear with my new silk dress. I haven't had a chance to wear it yet. Oh, I do hope for good weather. We can arrange for a new dress for you, Emmaline. What do you think you would like?"

As often happened, Jim and his sister Emmaline were of a like mind when dealing with their family. Emmaline actually grimaced at the thought of a new dress, and Jim's meal was turning over in his stomach at the thought of Olivia in Armsworth's clutches.

"I would like to stay home, but I doubt that will be possible," Emmaline replied.

"Heaven's sakes, Emmaline," Louise said, "Mr. Armsworth said that friends of his from the governor's office and some family friends would be attending as well as townsfolk. There's bound to be hordes of unattached, handsome young men. Why would you want to stay home?"

"How do you know they will be handsome?" Emmaline asked, clearly goading their mother.

"Look at Mr. Armsworth! Good Lord! He's a handsome man. No doubt his friends will be, too."

"Nettie told us she can't stop thinking about Mr. Armsworth in the buff," Emmaline said with a tittering laugh. "I suppose all the girls are thinking the same thing."

"Emmaline! How . . . I can't believe . . . I will speak to Nettie about this. Keep yourself to your room until you're prepared to apologize to me and your brother. How crass!" Louise pushed back her chair in a hurry and left the dining room without meeting her son's eyes.

"You've embarrassed Mother," Jim said.

Emmaline shrugged. "Perhaps Mother should be embarrassed by her constant badgering about my unmarried state."

"Did Nettie really say that?"

"She did," Emmaline said and stood. "She said it to me and Olivia and Marabelle and then was embarrassed that she'd said it aloud. But don't worry, brother. No one is thinking about *you* in the buff."

CHAPTER 4

"What is *he* doing here?" Olivia asked.

Her sister-in-law straightened her back and looked over her shoulder. "Jim? He's here to help Matt remove a stump."

Olivia bent back over the hoed row in the kitchen garden behind Matt and Annie's house. She dropped bean seeds as she slowly backed up. Annie followed, covering the seeds with loose soil and sprinkling water from a can. Thankfully they were nearly done. Olivia's dress was sticking to her with sweat and dirt, and she was looking forward to drawing a bath and afterwards lounging about in a cool dress on the back terrace. Away from Jim Somerset.

"I'd like to get the corn in, too, but if you want to go, don't worry a bit," Annie said and wiped her face with a less than pristine apron. "My goodness, it's a hot one for this early in June."

"I don't mind; it's going quickly since Sally took Teddy for his nap," Olivia said.

"It does go faster when we're not worried about him eating worms," Annie said with a laugh.

The two women worked in tandem, planting and covering three long rows of corn. Olivia was nearly out of the corn kernels she held in her apron when a shadow came over her, blocking the sun on her back, and she heard her brother's voice.

"Can't you two work any faster?"

Annie laughed. "Faster than the two of you standing there chawing like neither of you had a care in the world. We women-folk are always having to do more than our share."

Matt grabbed Annie from behind and swung her around, laughing and kissing the back of her neck as he did. "I did more than my share last night!"

"Matthew!" Annie said. "Dear Lord! Put me down and don't mention such things."

It took Olivia a minute to understand that her brother was referring to their intimate relations. Even in the summer sun, she felt her face flush. She refused to look to where Jim stood, just out of her line of vision. She'd rather look at Annie and Matt's joy than at Jim Somerset's misery, even if it did cause her to blush and imagine what kind of work was being done. She was tempted, though, feeling as if his eyes were on her, and as if he was tickling a feather up and down her arms and legs. She focused on her brother, now facing her and Jim, and still holding Annie loosely in his arms. They were the very picture of a happily married young couple. Olivia was so very glad for them both.

"Sally packed a picnic lunch for us, and there'll be plenty for the both of you, too. Come on, we'll go on down to the creek and play in the cool water," Matt said to them.

"Oh no," Annie said. "Teddy will be fussy in the sun so long and—"

Matt hugged her tightly and set his chin on her shoulder. "I've already told Sally we're taking a little holiday for ourselves today. She can handle Teddy for a few hours, and he was sound asleep just a minute ago."

"I feel strange asking Sally to help do those sorts of things," Annie said.

"She works for us, Annie," Matt said. "We pay her well above the going wage for housekeepers. She's not a slave."

"It does sound wonderful! A picnic and a wade in a creek."

Olivia smiled and brushed her hands together, happy to see both so content and in love. "I'll just be going then. Enjoy your picnic!"

"No!" Annie said. "Don't go so soon!"

"There's plenty, Livie," Matt said. "Come on! The water will be cold, though!"

Jim turned and walked away from them, raising a hand in farewell as he walked to his horse.

Matt straightened. "I never thought I'd live to see Jim Somerset be afraid of a little bit of water, but it looks like the older he gets the bigger the coward he is."

Jim stopped midstride, and Olivia watched his shoulders rise and fall with a deep breath. Just when she thought he'd succumbed to her brother's baiting, he continued walking to where his horse was standing under a tree, munching on grass.

Annie smacked Matt's arm and wiggled free. "Don't go, Jim," she said as she hurried to him. "Matt can be downright mean, and I'm sorry for it, but I don't want you to go. You've come all the way out here to help us and I don't want you to go away hungry. I'd feel terrible. Please say you'll stay!"

Jim turned to her, glanced at Olivia, and turned back to Annie. "Your husband can be a horse's ass, but I don't want to offend you, Annie."

Annie was all smiles as she turned to Olivia. "Say you'll stay, Livie?"

It seemed as though Annie would be frightfully disappointed if she left, and Olivia was hungry. Why was she being such a goose? If Jim Somerset wasn't here, she'd have already raced Matt to the creek. Why should she act any differently now?

"I'll be happy to stay for a bit. Mother wasn't expecting me at any particular time."

Annie clapped her hands together. "Wonderful!"

Olivia hooked arms with Annie, forestalling a walk through the woods with Jim by her side, and walked into the trees on a worn trail. The temperature dropped under the tree cover, and she could hear the gurgle of the stream in the distance.

"How nice on a hot day like this to get in the shade of these big oaks."

Olivia nodded and pulled close to her sister-in-law. "I love the woods," she said in a near whisper and gazed up at the thick ceiling of leaves. "There's something magical or spiritual about it, don't you think?"

"I could always think things through in the woods back home when I was a young girl. Sort things out. The war stopped that, of course. I was too afraid to leave our property once it started. Some days I was afraid to leave the cabin."

"I am so glad you are here now," Olivia said. "You're safe, and I never had a sister until now and didn't realize what I was missing."

"There was a healer named Gilly I would talk to some, who I'll most likely never see again. It's so good having a woman to talk to again. Speaking of talking, what's going on between you and Jim Somerset? And don't tell me 'nothing' again like you said the morning after the party at Paradise."

The women stepped into a sunny patch of grass beside a lone maple tree, its leaves swaying in the breeze and hanging over the creek. Jim was carrying blankets and Matt the picnic basket, well behind them on the trail. Olivia watched the men as they ambled along.

"He was my first love. Matt was always teasing me, and Adam too much older to dote on a young sister and busy helping my father with the horses. But Jim always found time for me. Even when I was young, not more than six or seven years old. He would have been about ten. I remember dragging him into the woods to a cave and showing him something I'd found. I think it was an arrowhead. He sat down on the ground beside me, cross-legged, and looked at it for a long time. Tilting his head and staring at it and at the cave where I'd found it. He was never dismissive of me and always took time to make me feel important and grown-up."

"What happened?" Annie said. "Why do you two circle each other like a skunk and a possum now?"

"He changed his opinion of me drastically as we got older. My champion was gone," Olivia said flatly. "Our friendship has been . . . uneasy, or rather over, ever since."

Matt was laughing when the two men walked up to where Olivia and Annie were standing. Annie spread a blanket, plopped down, and pulled her boots and stockings off, and Matt dropped his shirt and yanked his boots off.

"When did you dam this?" Olivia asked.

"A month or two ago. I figured it would be a good spot on a hot day or maybe on a hot night, too."

"Do you know this part of the creek?" Annie asked.

"Yes. I used to ride down here on my pony with Matt and Adam. The 'sister' tree is close by, and in the summer, we used to play in this creek, catching crawfish and wading."

"The 'sister tree'?" Annie asked.

"It happened the first time Daddy brought Mother here to Paradise after they were married. Mother's family had all been murdered not long before, and on the way back to Winchester she said she looked this way and saw a tree and her sister Ruth's face beside it. She called it the sister tree from then on," Matt said. "We've been playing here since we were kids and could walk or ride our ponies here, although it's not two hundred yards from Paradise as the crow flies."

"I couldn't imagine a prettier spot. Turn around now, boys. I want to untie my petticoats," Annie ordered.

Jim walked away alongside the creek bank, his back to the blanket, while Matt leaned against the maple with his eyes closed.

"No peaking!" Annie said with a laugh as she and Olivia pulled up their skirts and pulled off their cotton petticoats. Annie pulled her dress up between her knees and wrapped a cord around her waist to pull the skirts over. She was exposed from the knees down, but she wouldn't be constantly holding up her skirts, Olivia thought. How clever!

"Matt? There's another piece of cord in the basket. Give it to Olivia so she can hook her skirts on it," Annie said. "I want to get this jarred tea in the creek so it stays cold for our lunch."

Matt stumbled forward, his arm outstretched holding the twine in his fingers, as if he couldn't see where he was or where he was going. He dropped it near Olivia where she stood at the edge of the water. She belted it around her waist loosely and pulled her skirts up and over it.

"Oh no! I can't see," Matt said as he circled around and lurched to Olivia, arms out at his sides. He caught her around the waist and half dragged, half carried her to the water. He went in face-first, flat out, smacking his bare chest on the moving water while Olivia landed on her back and quickly submerged.

She came up out of the water, shaking her head, her hair flying around her, and shouting her brother's name. Matt was already standing in the waist-deep water, laughing and splashing her even as she wiped her eyes. She slammed her palms on the surface and caught him with a cascade of water in his face.

"You'll pay for that!" he shouted and charged at her.

Olivia whooped a laugh and ran as quickly as the water and her skirts would let her, out of the creek bed and onto the grass.

"Matthew! You've soaked your sister's clothes the whole way, and she's our guest!" Annie shouted.

He swept his arms around the surface of the water, sending a shower on his wife. She sputtered and laughed. "Oh my, does that feel good," she said and walked in the creek until she was beside him. He slouched down, up to his chin and pulled her down with him, slowly floating, their faces inches apart, talking and smiling. He kissed her cheek and grinned.

Olivia pulled her blouse out from the waistband of her skirt, unbuttoned it, and wrung out the tail, half tempted to pull it off and just wear her chemise. And then she remembered it wasn't just family on this picnic.

JIM WATCHED HER. HE COULDN'T HELP HIMSELF, EVEN THOUGH he knew he shouldn't. Her skirts were pulled up between her legs, exposing well-shaped rider's calves, muscled and smooth. She had pulled her wet hair up on top of her head and stuck a comb through it to hold it in place, leaving tendrils down her neck and back. Then she turned toward him. Her blouse was out of her skirt and unbuttoned, hanging open, the edges just touching the tips of her breasts. There was a silky white underthing covering her, with lace at the neckline and thin straps he could see. The wet fabric of it clung to her skin, to her breasts, leaving little to his imagination. It was all he could do to breathe. She looked up at him.

"Oh," she said.

But she didn't cover herself. He swallowed a growl and looked her in the eyes.

"Don't wait for us if you're hungry," Matt called out, breaking the spell Olivia had woven around him. "We're going for a walk."

Jim watched Matt help his wife out of the water on the opposite bank of the creek and sling an arm around her shoulders. She slid hers around his back. They walked, barefoot, Matt bare chested, to the woods. There was not a doubt in Jim's mind where they were going or what they'd be doing. He looked back at Olivia. She was the most beautiful woman he'd ever seen, and ever would see, he imagined. What would it be like to bed her whenever they pleased? Would it be heaven here on earth?

"Aren't you getting in the water?" she asked.

He shook his head.

"Well, I am. It's perfect, and I'm already getting hot again."

Jim watched her step over pebbles and rocks to the creek's edge, inching into the water, a shiver trailing over her back. She turned around and looked at him as she sank down in the water. Her blouse floated on the surface, her breasts as visible as if she were naked, her nipples hard points at the waterline.

"Isn't this big enough for the both of us? I'll gladly stay to my side, and you can stay over there near the dam."

He sat down and pulled off his boots and socks with trembling hands. He was fully erect and would have preferred to find some privacy to satisfy himself. But he could hardly excuse himself to trot off into the woods and stroke himself, Olivia's face floating in front of his closed eyes. He pulled his shirt over his head and walked into the water. He was satisfied to see her watch him, her eyes trailing over his bare chest and arms. He was far from vain, but he knew he was muscled and hard in all the places that women seemed to prefer. A few had even told him so. Emmaline told him if he wanted to find a wife, all he'd need to do was work the forge without his shirt. She said the women in town would riot to be his bride.

The water was cool and soothing and served to temper his ardor. He floated on his back in the middle of the slow-moving water where it was deepest. The sun was shining and the maple tree's leaves waved on a light breeze overhead as he concentrated on what the schedule was at the forge in the coming week, on conjugating Latin verbs, on anything to keep from thinking about Olivia Gentry, floating six feet away from him and now softly humming.

"What a lovely idea this was," she said quietly.

"Um huh."

"I wonder where Matt and Annie have gone? Neither of them had any shoes on."

Jim said nothing, just kicked his legs a few times to get moving. What was there to say in this case?

She stood up in the water and looked at the bank her brother and sister-in-law had climbed up. "You don't suppose something's happened, do you? Should we look for them?"

He turned to her and knelt in the water. "They're fine."

She nodded, stretched out on the water's surface and floated toward him with the current. "I suppose you're right." She looked at him then as if he was withholding a critical piece of information. "What do you think they're doing?"

He stared at her. "They're newly married. What do you think they're doing?" He couldn't keep the anger out of his voice.

A blush rose on her cheeks and spilled down to her chest where her breasts were rising in and out of the water's lazy flow.

"Oh."

"Oh, is right."

She swam away from him, slow strokes, and turned on her back. "There is no bed, though."

"I am absolutely certain your brother does not need a bed to . . ."

"To what?" she said, challenging him with her voice.

He swam to her, dunking his head to clear his thoughts before coming out of the water near her. "To have sexual congress. To copulate. To make love," he whispered.

She was staring at him then, staring at his mouth. She moved her eyes slowly to his, and her lips parted in invitation. He was breathing hard, barely controlling himself, knowing this was what he feared the most. He was terrified he'd scare her, maybe scare himself, with his lack of control.

"Aren't you the clever one? Perhaps you can detail the act in the original Latin," she said defiantly, although her cheeks flamed.

"I could."

Her eyebrows rose. "You've made a study of it, have you?"

"Just scholarly works."

"There are scholarly works?"

He nodded.

"Oh."

It was as if everything around them ceased to exist. The air quit its movement, the birds left off their chirping, and the water stopped its lapping. They moved in slow circles around each other, no more than a few feet apart. The water felt warmer to him suddenly, as if their bodies were heating it up even more than the sun's rays. His eyes were riveted to hers and hers to his and the only thing he could hear was the steady beat of his own heart. What would happen if he kissed her?

Olivia took one stroke toward him and touched her lips to his while the tips of her breasts grazed his chest. Their eyes met, making him unable to imagine this moment in time was nothing but a private dream. It was real and happening at that very second. He breathed in short gasps of air and felt his heart galloping along, making his blood rush to his fingertips and toes and to his cock.

She swam away quickly, her back to him. He had no earthly idea of what to say to her or why she'd kissed him, other than perhaps he had provoked the situation with his talk. Now he was too addled to do much of anything and was just glad he hadn't drowned in four feet of water.

Laughter from the opposite bank brought his head up.

MATT BURST OUT OF THE WOODS, RUNNING, AND JUMPED INTO the water, belly down, splashing her and making great waves of water. Annie followed him in at a leisurely pace and dunked her head back into the water to wet her hair completely.

"The woods were cool but not quite cool enough. This feels heavenly!" she said as she waded over to where Olivia stood. "If it was just you and I, we could swim in our shifts and not worry about these heavy skirts."

Olivia mumbled a response. She could not for the life of her understand what devil had possessed her to kiss Jim Somerset. All she knew was when he'd said those words in his low growl, she hadn't been able to think straight. Had lost all sense of who she was and what she wanted out of life. When her breasts had met his chest, his wet, hard, male chest, she'd nearly swooned and heat shot down her body to her private parts, making her lower belly ache with desire.

"Olivia?"

She turned when she heard her name and realized that Jim, Annie, and Matt had left the water. "Aren't you coming out to eat?" Annie asked.

Olivia walked out of the creek, squeezing the water from her hair and then from her skirts. Matt and Annie were sitting on the blanket. Matt was eating a piece of fried chicken, leaning back on one arm, his legs stretched out straight in front of him. Olivia noticed Jim standing at the tree line, his back to them.

"Sit down, Olivia," Annie said. "I've got buttermilk biscuits and cheese and plenty of chicken. Jim? Aren't you hungry?"

"He's always hungry," Matt said and picked up a biscuit that Annie had buttered. "He could eat three times as much as me as a kid." He turned his head and yelled over his shoulder, "I don't believe for one minute that you aren't hungry! Don't be insulting my wife by not eating your meal with us!"

"Leave him be," Annie said.

Jim walked over to the blanket and sat down on the grass near Annie. She handed him a jar of tea and fried chicken. He ate silently, staring across the water to the woods. Olivia looked at his profile and wondered what was going through his head. Probably thinking she was as forward and as unwanted as Marabelle. She was furious with herself! She'd gone and made herself look pitiful to him. *Again.*

"Did you hear about the fete to be held at Mrs. Barrett's home?" Annie asked Jim.

He nodded.

"There's already talk about it at Paradise," Matt said. "Mother and Aunt Brigid and Livie, and now my wife, too, fretting about what they'll be wearing. I'll get up that day and put on some clothes. I don't know why they can't do the same."

"Oh pooh," Annie said. "You'll not be wearing your work clothes. Don't act as if you will. And we've been talking about what to wear because we like to be pretty for our menfolk as much as we like to have new duds."

Matt glanced at her and smiled. "You're always pretty," he said to her and then leaned forward to speak to Jim. "I'll bet the goings-on at the Somerset house are just as frantic with four sisters and your mother. Well, Emmaline won't care, will she?"

Jim shook his head. "The others have been talking about it some."

Matt barked a laugh. "That's an understatement, I imagine."

"Have you decided what to wear, Olivia?" Annie asked. "Are you getting something made new?"

"No. I have something that will do. Maybe the peach taffeta."

"Quite an honor, with Mr. Armsworth asking you for the first dance," Annie said.

"What? You didn't tell me that, Annie," Matt said.

"Mr. Armsworth asked if he could lead me out for the first dance shortly after he invited everyone while we were at the Hospital Aid meeting." Olivia shrugged. "It's only a dance."

Jim harrumphed.

"I don't like it, and I'm going to say something to Mother," Matt said.

"You'll do no such thing," Annie said to her husband. "Olivia is well able to handle that gentleman or any other gentleman for one dance."

"You didn't see how close he was standing to her at the ball. I did," Matt said. "I don't like it."

"Mother knows he has asked me. If she hasn't stopped me, you won't be able to. And after all, Matt, we will be in full view of the citizens of Winchester. What could possibly happen?"

"Plenty can happen," he said and accepted the plate of cobbler that Annie handed him.

"I like Mr. Armsworth. He's gentlemanly and he's humorous.

Not silent and full of himself like some. I'm looking forward to dancing with him," she said and realized that what she had said was true. She was looking forward to the picnic and was happy to anticipate dancing with a handsome, smiling man. Not like the morose one sitting just off the blanket and staring into the woods.

"He's also very good-looking," Annie said with a laugh and turned to her husband, who raised his brows. "Not as good-looking as Matt Gentry, mind you, but he'll catch the eyes of plenty of ladies to be sure."

"It sounds as though we have competition, Somerset."

Jim nodded and continued to stare off in the distance. Olivia watched him for any further reaction, but there was none. She was suddenly, and irrationally, angry.

"Why are you even going to the picnic when you'll just be finding a patch of grass or a rock to sit on so you can judge the rest of us from afar?" she said to him.

Jim turned slowly to face her and stared at her until her cheeks reddened, although she had nothing to be ashamed of, did she? Other than throwing herself at him in the pond earlier. She looked away over her shoulder, unable to look at him and not remember every close detail when she'd kissed him. His heavy beard and thick neck and dark brown eyes, nearly black, under the shadow of his brow—and his broad, muscled chest.

"Where you going?" she heard Matt say and turned her head.

Jim had pulled his boots on and stood up. He touched his finger to his hat in Annie's direction. "Thank you for the delicious meal," he said and walked away on the path back to Matt's house.

Matt looked at Olivia and shook his head. He lay back on the blanket and put his hat over his face. She rose and followed the creek at its bank, wondering how she would ever reconcile her lingering and confusing feelings for Jim Somerset. She was desperate to move on with her life. To move forward and reach for great things as her family expected her to do, and find love as she expected for herself.

CHAPTER 5

"Where are my ribbons? Mother! Have you seen my ribbons?" Jane Somerset shouted from an upstairs hallway.

Jim shook his head where he sat in the kitchen of the main house, having come from his room behind the forge, now drinking his coffee and reading a week-old Richmond newspaper. Helen, the family cook, looked at the ceiling as if she could divine the detail of the mayhem now occurring on the second floor of the Somerset home, as she stirred a pot of something delicious-smelling on the stove.

"I'll be glad when this picnic is over," she said.

"No more than me," he replied.

"Betsy and Jane have themselves fit to be tied with worry about their gowns and their hair and such."

Emmaline walked in the kitchen door carrying an armload from the garden. "Here is everything you asked for," she said to Helen.

"Miss Emmaline! Put that all down and go get yourself a bath. You're meant to leave shortly for the picnic."

"I'll go in a minute. I can help you clean this cabbage before I do."

"You will not clean this cabbage," Helen said and took the knife from her hand. "Please, Miss Emmaline."

"Mother and your sisters will be disappointed if we're late," Jim said.

Emmaline blew out a breath and stormed out of the kitchen. Moments later, Jim could hear his mother shouting at her that she was going to make them all late with her tangled hair and dirty fingernails.

Some time later, Jim and Phillip mounted horses for the ride to Mrs. Barrett's, while his mother, Betsy, and Jane milled around the gig, pulling gloves tight and patting their hair one final time for stray strands. Emmaline took the reins and climbed in before he could help her, declaring that she was driving the horses and would concentrate on that so that she didn't have to listen to the nonsense coming out of her sisters' mouths. He could hardly blame her as Jane and Betsy hadn't not stopped to take a breath since midmorning.

He took his mother's hand as she stepped up to the seat. "You look very well, Mother. It is good to see you with color in your cheeks."

She turned to him once she was seated. "Thank you, Jim. You're a good son." She patted his face with her gloved fingers.

Jim handed his younger sisters up and complimented each of them on their frocks and hats, earning shy smiles from them both. Betsy kissed his cheek.

"I don't know why I'm so nervous," she said. But she smiled when she said it, and her cheeks were glowing. Betsy and Jane both looked very pretty and would be noticed at the fete. What would he do when suitors came around for them? It had been hard enough with Nettie even though he'd known John Winders for years. Those two had had starry eyes for each other since they were fourteen years old. It was no surprise when John asked to speak to him as the head of the family, but it had still been hard.

It was Nettie. His closest companion growing up, with only a few years between them.

Emmaline was a different story. He wondered if she'd grow old as a prop to their mother. She never bothered with her appearance, had a deadly sense of humor and wasn't afraid to use it on those she deemed unworthy. She would not be "easy" for any man.

Emmaline turned to her sisters. "Have you two quit your fussing and squirming? I'm going to haw these horses, and if you don't want to fall out of the gig, you'd better hang on."

Jane and Betsy grabbed the side rails as Emmaline did just that. He could hear their mother complaining that her hair was being blown about and to slow down. He trotted along beside his family, greeting others headed in the same direction and chatting with them about the upcoming day and the graciousness of Mrs. Barrett and her nephew. Jim thought if he didn't hear one more word about the fabulous Mr. Armsworth, of the broad shoulders and the golden hair, he could die a happy man.

He gazed into the woods and did his best not to listen to the raptures about Armsworth. He knew there was something irrational about his impatience, and if he was honest with himself, anger, for Richard Armsworth. The man was, after all, a new entity in a town that had few strangers or newcomers in its ranks, especially handsome, well-educated ones. It was within reason for folks to fuss a bit over him. So why did he dislike the man so much? He swallowed. As much as he liked to shy away from the obvious reason, he had to face the fact that his enmity sprang mostly from Armsworth's actions toward Olivia Gentry.

And there she was again, at the forefront of his thoughts, even as he did his best to push her to the back of his mind. But why then, when he closed his eyes at night, did he envision her in the creek, just feet away from him, her hair slicked back from her face and her chest glistening with water and sunshine. Olivia Gentry was, and always would be, a lady, both in thought and deed as far as he was concerned; why then could he only see her as a seductress?

He'd been seduced by her looks when she'd glanced at him with wide, innocent eyes when she was just fifteen years old. She'd gone away to a finishing school or a college, he didn't remember which, shortly after that. She'd come home a year and a half later as the most beautiful female he'd ever set on eyes and ever would. At seventeen, she was an inch taller, a few inches rounder at the bosom and hips,

and more self-possessed than any other young woman of his acquaintance. He'd been hypnotized by her. And she was his best friend's younger sister who looked at him as a protector. He could never betray Matt's trust in him to be honorable.

OLIVIA HAD TRIED ON THE PEACH TAFFETA AND SHRUGGED OUT of it. She'd always thought it brought out the red in her hair and the pale freckles across her nose which were hardly visible otherwise, other than when she'd spent too much time in the sun without her hat. She stuck her head in her hanging closet, peering in the back, finally seeing the moss green silk she'd had made earlier in the year. The bodice was fitted and rather low-cut although not immodest, with airy lace sleeves in the same color to her elbow with a pointed cuff and paste dangles in green. She wore a light bustle and one silk petticoat under the skirt, which draped and moved elegantly with lace about the hem. The underskirt was pleated moss green silk with gauzy overskirts draped open atop it to reveal the silk.

Beatrice, the upstairs maid, poked her head through the door. "You've asked for me, Miss Olivia?"

"Yes, Beatrice," she said as she turned. "I thought you might do something with my hair today. Something up off my neck that will still accommodate this little hat." She examined the felt and silk creation in her hand.

Beatrice went to work with the curling tongs and pins, making an elaborate, loosely braided knot just above her neck. The hat was pinned into place above it, and Olivia looked left and right at her reflection. She was in good looks, she thought to herself; the green complemented her skin and eyes and the dress was flattering and feminine.

She thought briefly of how she'd looked when she'd arrived home from playing in the creek at Annie and Matthew's. She was thankful her mother hadn't seen her come in the kitchen door and take the back steps to her room. When she'd pulled off her blouse and turned to her mirror, she'd seen herself as they'd seen her, as Jim Somerset had seen her, in her still damp chemise that clung to every curve of her breasts and was nearly transparent. It was one more mortification to add to that day, she thought.

But she wouldn't think of that day or the way that Jim had looked at her or how his lips and mustache had felt against her mouth. She was going to enjoy herself. She was going to dance the opening set of dances with the host of an outdoor fete in a beautiful setting. And he was a handsome man. Didn't all the ladies say so?

* * *

ADAM HELPED HIS MOTHER DOWN FROM THE GIG WHEN THEY arrived at Barrett House, and a servant helped Olivia climb down the one metal step. The gig was taken by a young man and moved around the long, graveled drive behind a long line of other conveyances. Olivia wondered how big the carriage house was at Barrett House to accommodate all the horses and all the buggies that would be bringing guests to the party. She turned to view the stately brick house when Richard Armsworth himself made his way down the wide steps from the portico, smiling and welcoming them. He went directly to Mother and bent over her hand. She could hear his introduction to Adam. Armsworth walked to where she stood and looked at her as if there were no other carriages arriving and no other sounds of activity nearby. He smiled and bent to kiss her outstretched hand.

"My long wait is finally over," he said. "I am so glad you have arrived, Miss Gentry."

Olivia smiled. She couldn't help herself if what he implied was true—that he'd been waiting for her among all his guests. Why shouldn't she smile in any case? He was a handsome man and he was wrapping her hand about his arm and leading her up the steps. He turned to Adam and Mother.

"Allow me to show you where the food and drinks are and the ladies' retiring room in case you've a hem that is sagging or need a moment to recover from your ride here," he said. "Follow me."

"There are others arriving that you will want to greet, Mr. Armsworth. I'm sure we can make our way inside," Olivia said.

He bent his head to hers. "The staff here at Barrett House are very good and will greet newcomers and help them find their way just as they have been doing since the very first guest arrived. Can you imagine who the first guest was?"

"Mayor Fitzhugh would be my guess. But you distract me." She stopped and pulled her arm from his to face him and noticed Mother and Adam being led inside by Mrs. Barrett. "I'm sure you need to see to your other guests."

He grinned. "Would you like to greet them with me?"

She shook her head but couldn't hold back a smile. "No, Mr. Armsworth. Of course not. It would appear that I . . ."

"Am an honored guest. You are."

She looked down at her hands. He really was very persuasive and charming, she thought, and she was here to enjoy herself. She looked up at him, a half smile playing on her face.

"Would you be so kind as to show me where the beverages are? I'm quite thirsty, and I may need to find the ladies' retiring room as I believe there is a snag in my lace glove."

"Horror of horrors! A snag! Allow me," he said with a chuckle and offered his arm.

They walked together through the cool hallways of the house past other guests, many of whom Armsworth begged her to formally introduce him to. She was the subject of several speculative glances, she knew, but was enjoying his company far too much to mind.

"There you are, Olivia," Matt said as he and Annie approached. "We've been looking for you. Annie wants to show you the collectibles Mrs. Barrett has laid out for guests to see." He offered his arm, but Olivia didn't move.

"I'm sorry to say I haven't had the pleasure." Armsworth looked first at Annie and then at Olivia.

"Mrs. Annie Gentry, wife of my older brother, Matt. She's originally from Bridgewater. I believe you and Matt were acquainted on the night of the Paradise ball."

"Mrs. Gentry, so pleased that you've come," he said and looked at Matt but continued speaking to Annie. "Your husband took exception to how close I was standing to his sister that evening. He was quite right. I've apologized but I don't think that has convinced him that my attentions are entirely honorable." He gave Annie a quick smile. "Perhaps you can take up my cause."

"He can be awful stubborn and worries about his sister." Annie held on to Matt's arm. "I'll find you later to look at Mrs. Barrett's things, Olivia, when Matt's playing horseshoes."

"We can look at them now, if you wish. Will you join Miss Gentry and me? Will your husband release you?" Armsworth asked as he smiled broadly at Annie and winged his arm.

Annie glanced up at Matt and slid her arm free of his. "He'd rather talk with the men than look at silver cups and whatnot. I believe I'll join you."

"I am the luckiest man today! Two beautiful women! One for each arm. Where is a portrait painter when one needs one?"

Armsworth said as he led Olivia and Annie down the hall. Both women laughed.

"He's slicker than horse snot," Matt said to no one in particular.

"He is at that," Adam said as he came to stand beside his brother. "But he's a handsome devil if you listen long enough to the women. Stole your bride right out from under your nose."

Matt cast a sidelong glance at Adam. "Not likely, brother. Annie is loyal to a fault. Anyway, she knows I've already killed men defending her. I'd do it again in an instant."

"I know. I was right there beside you if you remember. It's just that when a woman looks up at a man like Annie did to Armsworth, it can make you wonder if you can still make her as starry-eyed as he did. Maybe you're losing your touch."

"Don't try and goad me," Matt said quietly. "I know what you're doing. I won't take the bait." He stared down the long hallway and frowned. "Maybe I better go join them, though. It's only polite."

"Where's Matt off to?" Jim Somerset said to Adam.

"Mrs. Barrett has displayed some collectibles and antiquities she brought from London for today's guests to view," Adam replied as he watched his brother walk quickly down the wide, carpeted hallway. "Mr. Armsworth has escorted Livie and Annie to see them. I believe Matt has decided he should be there when they faint away over Armsworth's blue eyes."

Adam turned to face Jim and his younger sisters, one on each arm. "Well! When did these two lovely young ladies grow up? How beautiful you both look today!"

Betsy smiled, and Jane giggled. "It is such a lovely party, don't you think? The house is beautiful, and the food, my goodness, there are enough cakes and fruit to last a week and a day!" Betsy said and then blushed. "Mother warned me to hold my tongue but I just can't seem to stop myself."

"I agree with you wholeheartedly, Betsy," Adam said with a smile. "Are you looking forward to the dancing?"

JIM STARED DOWN THE HALLWAY TO THE DOORWAY MATT HAD just gone through. Adam was charming his sisters, who were as giddy as he'd ever seen them. He'd watched Armsworth enter the house through the big double doors standing open for guests, pausing just inside with Olivia on his arm. They'd been laughing and talking, his head bent to hers. Everyone loitering in the grand hallway entrance had turned to watch them, some sly, some openly staring. He'd stared, too, he admitted to himself. He would say they were a handsome couple when he was able to look at them objectively. But how could he be objective about Olivia Gentry? She was a young woman falling for the smooth charm of a man who sought out those he could gain the most from. He looked at his sisters, still talking to Adam, although he'd missed most of their conversation.

"Would you like to go see Mrs. Barrett's things?" he asked.

"What's put you in the mind to drag these two nincompoops to see some old plates?" Emmaline asked as she joined them.

"Maybe Jim has an interest in the artifacts," Adam said and stared at him, making him feel as if the man knew exactly why he'd offered to escort his sisters.

Betsy and Jane linked arms with him and propelled him forward even though he needed little prompting. Adam and Emmaline watched them go.

"I don't believe he understands himself yet," Emmaline whispered.

"Neither does she," Adam murmured.

JIM STOOD LOOKING AT THE COLLECTION OF BOOKS THAT LINED the walls of Mrs. Barrett's library. He'd been standing there for near a half hour while Armsworth pointed out objects on the cloth-covered tables to Annie, Betsy, Jane, and, of course, Olivia, whose hand was wrapped firmly about his forearm. He had all four women laughing, or giggling in Jane's case, although he treated both girls well and included them in his questions and conversations, addressing them individually for their opinions. Jim heaved a breath. He would have to listen to Betsy and Jane talk about Armsworth for months after this interlude.

He put down the book in his hand and walked to where Armsworth was holding court. "Mother will be wondering where you've gotten to," he said to Betsy and Jane.

"I've monopolized your time, and I'm sure there is more than one young buck here waiting for his chance to speak to such lovely young ladies as the Misses Somerset," Armsworth said.

"I'll go with you, too, Jim," Annie said. "Matt was here, but he's taken off somewhere. I should find him."

Jane groaned, but both girls nodded and looked so forlorn he nearly changed his mind and let them stay—but it was true. His mother would be looking for them. They walked out of the library on either side of him, casting longing glances over their shoulders. Annie saw Matt across the wide lawn on a patio surrounded by blooming rosebushes and hurried to him. Jim found his mother talking to Mrs. Gentry, left the girls in her charge, and wandered off to the woods ahead, past the newly dug horseshoe pit where several men were already stripped of their jackets or vests waiting for their turn to play. Someone hollered to him, but he continued toward a path that led into the trees.

He walked on until he came to a painted bench set against a rhododendron overlooking a valley between the foothills that surrounded the house. The field was filled with wildflowers and was the sort of picturesque setting one read about in books, he thought. It was almost too perfect and beautiful to be true, much like what he thought about Richard Armsworth. Jim veered off the path and came to a large, flat rock. He stretched out on it and listened to the babble of a distant brook. He stared up at the slivers of blue sky peeking through the trees overhead. He should be happy for her.

She was clearly enthralled by Armsworth, and he with her. She would, no doubt, advance Armsworth's career at the capital, as only bright, beautiful spouses could. She would host parties and sway opinions and influence power brokers and be as successful as any woman could these days. She would be happy. He'd never pictured himself as a sad person, with regrets he'd not be able to overcome, who carried an unrequited love to his grave. But it appeared he might be exactly that person. He was having some difficulty being in the same room as the two of them and not shouting at her to come to her senses. To come to him. She had kissed him, though, that day in the creek. What did that mean? A playful gesture to an old friend?

He sat up, arms on his knees, and thought he'd best get back to the party. He couldn't hide forever, or even until the end of the day when he could escort his family home. And then he heard voices from near the bench on the other side of the bushes.

"The governor needs to discourage the Readjusters. Virginia needs freedmen to work, and at the wages we can pay."

"The governor was elected by the people he serves," Armsworth replied.

"The people that elected him expect him to get us our labor back."

"He doesn't have the support in the western parts of our newly divided state. When he has that, the Readjusters will never form in earnest or go away quietly if they have."

"Ha! So that's why you chase this Winchester girl so adamantly. You're setting the stage for bringing Winchester and other localities around to the Conservatives' point of view."

"Miss Gentry is lovely and well-bred and comes from a well-known, successful family. It is no hardship to pursue her, and an alliance with her family will only gain me credibility in this area of Virginia."

Jim sat quietly and listened as Richard Armsworth and another man continued walking and talking. He waited until he could no longer hear their voices. There was nothing inherently wrong with what Armsworth had said. Olivia was in possession of all the advantages he'd spoken of, and Armsworth wasn't the only man in history who'd pursued a woman and married her for what she could bring to him, be it a herd of cattle, a fortune, or political capital. But there was something in his tone, something dismissive, even as he spoke highly of her, that made anger bubble up from Jim's gut.

OLIVIA AND ARMSWORTH LEFT THE LIBRARY COLLECTION, stopping by the dining rooms for a lemonade before wandering out to the lawns. Groups of people stood together talking and a few were gathered at several tables enjoying a meal in the shade. There was a lovely cool breeze countering the warmth of the sun as they walked onto the grass. Armsworth led her to three men standing away from Winchester citizens. She did not recognize them.

"Miss Olivia Gentry, gentlemen," Armsworth said as he touched the back of her hand where it lay on his sleeve. "Allow me to introduce you to some gentlemen I work with at the governor's behest. Mr. Jeremy Sprangler, Mr. Nathan Beldman, and Mr. Louis Armond."

The gentlemen collectively nodded and smiled at her.

"Are you enjoying your day, Miss Gentry?" Mr. Armond asked.

"I am. Very much. The setting is beautiful, is it not?" she said.

"The landscape is very beautiful," Armsworth said as he looked around the clipped lawns beyond the patios and past them to the green foothills bordering Barrett House. "But the real beauty is much closer"—he turned his head to look at her—"close enough to touch."

Her face colored with embarrassment at his extravagant praise as the men assembled looked at her closely. She could imagine them thinking that Armsworth had touched her more than the gentlemanly linking of arms. She didn't care for the implication even if he hadn't meant it that way.

"Tell me, gentlemen, what do you think of the governor's balancing act between the Radical Republicans and the True Republicans?" Olivia asked.

The three men in front of her stared at her, their smiles fading, their eyes drifting off to the drinks in their hands or the landscape they'd just spoken of. Armsworth looked down at her, a tight smile on his face.

"My dear! What an interesting topic. We were just mentioning the new hat styles worn by so many of the ladies in Richmond. Have you seen them yet?" Armsworth asked her.

"Hats?" Olivia asked. "I was hoping to hear these gentlemen's opinions on Readjusters and Funders. I've read several articles but it's hard to parse what is actually proposed in the news . . ."

Mr. Sprangler and Mr. Beldman signaled to someone across the lawn, tipped their hats to her, and walked away.

"This is not a topic for a lady's ears," Armond said, staring at her with a frown.

"Are ladies not to understand what goes on in their country's government?" she asked.

"Really, Olivia," Armsworth said impatiently. "This is not a subject for a party."

"But when I joined you, the gentlemen were discussing a legislative issue."

Armond brushed at his sleeve casually. "Get your woman under control, Armsworth. This kind of independence does not flatter her *or* you."

Olivia watched the man walk away. She was too furious to

speak rationally and too embarrassed to reply. She turned to Armsworth, red-faced and seething.

"How unbelievably rude!" Olivia said.

"That man has the ear of the governor! What were you thinking?"

It took a moment for her to realize that Armsworth was as angry as she was. And his anger was focused on her! "What was I thinking? I was interested in hearing about something going on at our capital from men with firsthand knowledge."

Armsworth took a deep breath and looked over her head at the crowd. "I have no wish to call attention to us. Please lower your voice and smile."

"I'm not a trained monkey."

He glared at her, and for just a brief second, she was frightened by what she saw in his eyes. He was murderously angry.

"Let us walk a bit," he said finally.

They walked in silence, his hands behind his back and hers clasped at her waist.

"Armond is a man whose influence with the governor is great. I need to cultivate his opinion of me. It is vital to my career. To my future," he said and looked down at her, speaking in a normal tone of voice in contrast to the harshness of his previous comments.

"You may continue to cultivate his opinion, Mr. Armsworth, but I have no need of his good opinion. None at all."

He stopped walking and turned to face her, glancing up as he did. "The doctor and his wife are bearing down on us so I will speak quickly. Isn't it possible my future is also yours? Wouldn't my career benefit us both?"

"Ah, there you are Armsworth," Dr. Carter said as he and his wife, Madeline, walked toward them. "What a fine day this is! The grounds are beautiful and the food delicious! Weren't we just saying so, my dear," he said and glanced at his wife.

"Yes, you did—" she began.

"And your aunt! What a delight! Madeline and I were so entertained with her display from her home in London!"

As usual, Dr. Carter spoke over his wife, who smiled indulgently at him. Olivia could barely comprehend the conversation, though, as her mind was still turning Armsworth's words over in her head. 'My future also yours . . . benefit us both." The words were tumbling through her brain and she arrived repeatedly at the same conclusion. His words were a declaration—a very clear one. He was courting her, and she was not quite prepared for that thought even knowing that she'd looked forward to his company today. It was all very sudden and based on just a few brief interludes other than today, of course, which felt very much like his plan had succeeded and she had complied.

"Oh, do excuse me," she said interrupting Dr. Carter. "My mother is looking for me. Thank you so much for your escort, Mr. Armsworth."

Olivia walked away as if she knew the exact location of her mother. She saw Matt and Annie and strode toward them with purpose.

"Where is Mother?" she asked.

"Inside I think," Matt said.

"What is the matter?" Annie asked. "You're so pale!"

"Nothing. I would just like to talk to her is all. I'll go inside and find her," she said and walked toward the house. Annie caught up with her and slipped an arm through hers.

"I'll help you find her," she said and smiled.

Olivia stopped walking. "I'm fine. Really."

"You look like you've stepped on a grave, Livie."

"I just want to find Mother. I . . . I need to talk to her. I . . . Am I that gullible, Annie? Maybe Matt is right. Maybe I need a guardian, when all the other women my age are married and having babies."

"Your mother is over there," Annie said with a nod of her head. "She's talking to some town ladies."

Olivia looked over her shoulder and saw her mother speaking with six or seven women from the Ladies Hospital Aid and Recovery. She was not going to insert herself in that conversation.

"Come on," Annie said. "Let's walk, unless you're hungry. I never had roasted chicken as good. And the raspberry cake! Oh my!"

She let herself be led by Annie's linked arm across the lawn and around the side of Barrett House, now shady and nearly deserted. Annie talked on about the party and the food, but she heard little of it. She did sit down beside her sister-in-law on a bench tucked between lilacs, now faded but still fragrant. She looked up across the lawn toward the carriage house and thought about leaving the party at that instant.

"Mr. Armsworth believes we are courting."

Annie turned her head sharply. "That was quick, wasn't it? What did he say?"

"I said something to someone he was trying to impress, which that man did not care for, and Armsworth asked if I didn't realize that his future may also be mine. I was so stunned I could barely speak. We met at the Paradise ball, and again at the Ladies Hospital meeting. I agreed to dance the first dance with him at his picnic, and then he met us at the door when we arrived. I've been with him all afternoon. Everyone will draw the same conclusions as he has."

"It does seem hurried-like, but then what do I know. I wasn't brought up to know what the courting rules are. Do you like him?"

"He's charming. He's smart. He's very handsome. Yes, I do like him I suppose, but I'm terrified I'll fulfill my family's low expectations for my ability to navigate suitors. Mr. Dunderage will haunt me for quite some time, I think."

"You do like him *you suppose*? Does he make your insides quiver when he's near? Do you count the hours until you see him again?" Annie said with a dreamy look in her eyes. "I counted the minutes, the seconds, until I saw your brother again, until I thought I'd never see him again and then I thought I was going to die. I thought my heart would just stop beating."

Olivia shook her head and looked away. "No. Nothing like that. Not everyone's as lucky as you and Matt."

"There's never been anyone like that for you?"

She opened her mouth to deny it but could not. "A long, long time ago, there was someone like that for me. Not anymore."

Annie stood and smiled down at her. "Come. Let's go raid this dining room. Strawberries with chocolate sauce has to cheer you up!"

Olivia laughed with a cheerfulness she didn't feel. "You're right. I wish I didn't have to dance the first dance with him tonight, but that's hardly enough to make me miss strawberries and chocolate sauce!"

* * *

THE SUN HAD JUST SET BUT THERE WAS STILL AN HOUR OF daylight to be had. Servants had hung lanterns in the surrounding trees and planted tall torches around a wooden dance floor constructed wholly for the event. Musicians tuned their instruments when Mr. Armsworth approached her as she stood with her mother. He smiled his charming smile, not at all reminiscent of the look he'd given her after she spoke to his friends.

"I believe this is my dance," he said, after nodding to her mother.

"It is, thank you," she said with a smile and met his eyes. She laid her hand on his arm and went up the two steps to the dance floor as the orchestra began a waltz. He was a polished dancer, and she was intent on enjoying herself and letting the afternoon's upsetting episode fade into the background.

But she was soon distraught again as she noticed no other dancers had joined them. Armsworth was staring at her intently, and she realized she was the object of every guest's eyes. She looked up at him anxiously when she noticed his friend Nathan Beldman speaking to Matt and Annie as they started up the steps to the dance floor. It was almost as if Mr. Beldman was keeping her brother and sister-in-law from joining them. It was almost as if he wanted the dance to have a significant meaning to them . . . as a couple. She was embarrassed and provoked, especially when she noticed him raise a brow to the orchestra conductor just as Matt and Annie stepped onto the dance floor. The music wound down quickly and he stopped, made a short bow, and kissed the back of her hand all while staring at her intently. The crowd watching clapped and cheered as if it were a bridal dance. She could feel a blush rise up her face and over her chest. She forcibly stopped herself from running across the dance floor and down the steps. She would not allow herself to appear garish, or ill-mannered, even if her inclination was to slap Armsworth's face and run away, her skirts flying behind her.

Armsworth pulled her hand around his arm to escort her from the floor, and she allowed it. She withdrew her hand as soon as her feet were on grass and walked out of the crowd surrounding the dance floor at an unhurried pace. She hoped that he didn't try and catch up with her. She felt as if she would like to walk into the woods and walk and walk until she came out the other side in another county, or even another state.

Twilight had descended, though, and she wasn't walking into the woods, where tree cover had already made it dark. But she was heading toward the woods, where she could skirt the cool edges, away from the crowds until her breathing and sense were restored. She noticed two things as she walked. The sound of human voices had dimmed, and Jim Somerset was standing directly ahead of her.

"Of all people," she said softly.

He pushed off the tree he was leaning against and walked toward her. He didn't stop until he was standing close to her.

"Are you engaged to him?"

She shook her head. "No."

"What did that kiss mean?" he blurted out.

"I didn't kiss him," she said and looked so forlorn, so lost, that he wanted to gather her in his arms like he would a sister or brother who'd skinned a knee. But that wasn't quite true, or even true a small amount, because he wanted to ease her to the ground and cover her body with his. He wanted to touch her face and hair. He wanted to put his lips on hers.

"At the creek when you kissed me," he clarified.

She was silent for so long he wondered if she'd heard him or was ever going to answer if she had heard him. He was staring at her, waiting, when the tears began to roll down her cheeks and drop off her chin. The muscles in his chest contorted and twisted as he watched each tear fall. He had to force himself to breathe. Her hurt, her pain, was constricting his heart's ability to beat and his lungs' capacity to draw air and he understood at that moment with some clarity what poets meant by heartbreak.

"I'm such a fool," she whispered, her voice reedy. "I didn't mean for the dance to be . . . what it was." She looked up at him then, eyes wide with despair. "It was a beautiful day. I didn't mean to be forward. I . . . I never should have . . . It was just a kiss."

"Don't cry," he said softly. "I can't abide it." He wiped her chin and cheeks with his hand, large and rough and trembling uncontrollably against her pale, perfect skin.

"Livie?" he heard from over her shoulder.

"She's here, Adam," he said.

Olivia wiped her eyes and turned to her brother. "Can we go, Adam? I'm so tired. Can we please go home?"

"Of course, Livie. Mother is ready, too, I believe."

Jim watched her hurry to her brother's side. Adam pulled her close to him and kissed the top of her head.

CHAPTER 6

"Mrs. Barrett and her nephew are downstairs, Olivia. I'd like you to join us," her mother said. "Adam is with them now."

"I don't really care to see him, Mother," she said from the desk in the small sitting room beside her bedroom. She'd been staring out of the window that early September day, noting a few leaves changing color. "Perhaps they will be gone before you go down again."

Eleanor tilted her head. "Olivia? That is no way to act. We are ladies even when it is difficult to be one."

She stood, resigned to and expecting this moment for some time. "Of course, you are right, Mother." Olivia followed her down the stairs and into the main room, which served as the formal parlor. Richard Armsworth and Adam stood as they did.

"How good to see you, Mrs. Barrett!" Olivia said and smiled. She sat down in a chair near Mrs. Barrett and looked up at Armsworth. "Mr. Armsworth. It is a pleasure to see you again."

He smiled charmingly. "It has been far too long, Miss Gentry. I hope you've been well."

"I have. Thank you for asking."

"You've recovered, then, from your ailment during the last

Ladies Hospital Aid meeting. We missed you, dear," Mrs. Barrett said.

"It was nothing serious, just a headache, but I didn't feel up to the ride," she said.

"We're glad you've decided to visit your aunt's home again, Mr. Armsworth. How long will you be staying?" Eleanor asked.

Armsworth was staring at her as he spoke to her mother, but Olivia kept her eyes trained on Mrs. Barrett. She was able to smile and be friendly, even when she didn't feel that way, because she'd been brought up to be a lady, she said to herself over and again. She was no longer angry with him. That was long gone, but she'd found herself wary of others over the last few months, even so much as to keep to her rooms or the grounds of Paradise rather than attending meetings or shopping or socializing. She was angry with herself for hiding away. She looked up when she realized Mr. Armsworth was standing in front of her.

"Would you be willing to walk with me in your gardens, Miss Gentry?"

She took a deep breath and glanced at her brother's worried face and to her mother's calm one. "Certainly. My wrap is still in the hallway, I believe."

She walked out the door ahead of him, holding the ends of her shawl together at her waist. She had no intention of taking his arm.

"I believe I owe you an apology," he said as they took the stone walk that led to the back of the house.

"You may believe whatever you wish, Mr. Armsworth."

He looked down, stopping when they had walked around the corner of the house, out of sight, she noticed, of any windows of the main room. He faced her, and she looked up at him.

"I am sorry, Miss Gentry. I think those are the words you are looking for."

"For what are you apologizing, sir?"

He licked his lips. "You will not make this easy," he said with a forced laugh. "I suppose that should be expected from a young lady as well educated and confident as yourself. Ladies do not speak of matters of state or government at the capital, or in any of the good homes I've been privy to. It was surprising and caught both myself and Armond off guard." He paused and looked into her eyes with all the charm he'd been noted for. "But I never should have tried to silence you or speak over you. I should have told Armond that you may speak about anything you wish to speak about."

"Mr. Armsworth. I have been raised in a household where I was educated to the same degree as my brothers. Consulted even at a young age for my opinion. I have read about women who serve as academics in colleges and travel the country arguing for their causes. I have read about women who are inventors and scientists and mathematicians and doctors. I am involved in the decisions that are made in relation to our family business and investments. There is no reason to believe that I will suddenly stop reading or thinking or asking questions."

Mr. Armsworth had the good sense to look chagrined. "I suppose that is true."

"I don't care for manipulation, either," she said and stared at him.

His eyes slid away from hers, and she began walking again. They walked around the back of the house and she seated herself on the painted bench near the bricked patio. Armsworth propped a booted foot on the bench and leaned on his knee. He was looking serious with some expectancy.

"You are formidable, Miss Gentry. I am truly sorry that I made you in any way uncomfortable or focused unwanted attention in your direction on the day of the picnic. I have been gone from my aunt's since shortly after that day and had planned on calling on you before I left. If truth be known, I wasn't sure of my reception."

She raised her eyebrows to him. *Ah.* He had known then. He had known his behavior was shameful.

"I left without seeing you to make amends and have tormented myself about my cowardice ever since. This month, I arranged to do some of the governor's business in the western half of the state so that I might come back to my aunt's and try to put myself back in your good graces."

It was a pretty speech. All of it. He had said everything she would have wanted him to say. She did like his company, found him charming and handsome. Should she ignore that whisper in her head, her conscience or her father's ghost, that said Richard Armsworth was a dressed-up version of Timothy Dunderage?

She understood herself enough to know that she had lost her confidence, and even though others might see her as wealthy and educated and fortunate, which she was, she was still fragile and unsure of how her future would unfold. Any man she married or fixed on would be a central part of that future. Would define in society's eyes whether her hopes and dreams were fulfilled, whether her personal happiness and the draw of competency and ambition she had for herself would cross paths.

She supposed that she should end her self-imposed exile. What good did it do her to hide in her room? She'd answered some of her own questions in the last four months. She did wish to marry. She wanted children of her own. She wanted a companion, a man, all for herself, not meant to be shared with others. She wanted to experience intimacy, and although she could do that outside the bounds of marriage, she couldn't imagine it. How could one achieve the intimacy necessary to complete the act with a person that one had no relationship with, either from personal choice or law?

The final question, of course, was whether she would achieve any of those goals if love wasn't evident. Her mother and father hadn't been in love when they married. Yet they had grown to love each other and built a successful life together. Olivia believed that she could do as many other women had done before. Marry with purpose. Marry to achieve goals. Marry, not for love, but for compatibility and future hopes.

Mr. Armsworth was still staring at her. She looked down at her hands to take one final steadying breath and placed two feet into a new and unknown arena.

"What are you plans for your stay in Winchester?"

"I was hoping to stay for a few weeks at my aunt's and travel to towns close enough to be reached in a few hours for my work."

"There is to be a harvest dance in town this Saturday."

Armsworth smiled at her, his blue eyes flashing. "Would you allow me to escort you to the harvest dance, Miss Gentry?"

"I will be attending with my brother Adam and my mother. But I would be . . . pleased to meet you there."

"And reserve me a dance or two?"

"There is an informal supper served at the church between the fair and the dance. Perhaps you would like to dine with my family. I will reserve a seat for you, and your aunt, if you wish."

"I would be honored," he said and smiled at her in such a way that she was compelled to smile back. "We've been alone longer than your mother would consider proper. Allow me to escort you into the house."

"DID YOU HEAR THAT ARMSWORTH IS BACK IN TOWN?" Emmaline Somerset said to her brother.

Jim shook his head and looked back down at the columns of figures representing the farrier business's income and expenses for the year. He tallied a row of figures for the third time, coming up with a different answer for each, while Emmaline leaned against the door of his rooms behind the forge.

"Nothing to say?" she prodded.

He shook his head again.

"Good God!" she said in a near shout. "What will it take for you to come out of this cloud you've been in for months? Should I set my hair on fire?"

He looked up at her, hoping his silence would prompt her to leave as it had in the past. Today she wore a particularly stubborn face and was staring at him, breathing hard, her arms folded across her chest.

"You're going to live your life in this sad state, with this cloud of despair hanging about you, aren't you?"

He continued to stare at her, absorbing her words and knowing in some corner of his mind that they were true and that that truth hurt. His lips pursed and tightened but he said nothing.

"We should call you the gloom man. The man who will spend his life pining for a woman that—"

"That what?" he bellowed. "What damn thing is it that you want me to say that will get you to leave me alone!"

The moment the words were out of his mouth he wished he could take them back. He watched Emmaline's mouth close slowly and a flush cover her cheeks. She shook her head and opened the door.

"Wait," he said. "Wait. I'm sorry. I should not have spoken to you in that voice."

She looked at him with concern. "You've got to do something, Jim. I love you too much to see you in this state. You've always been quiet, but now you are silent. You've been contemplative, but now you are morose. I'm worried about you and so are mother and Nettie. Even Phillip asked me what was wrong with you, and that boy hasn't noticed anyone or anything but his own comfort for as long as he's been alive."

"I don't . . . I don't know what to say. I've been quiet lately, but I just had nothing to say."

Emmaline sat down in the chair beside his desk and looked at him with such pity that he had to turn his head. He shrugged.

"When are you going to fight for her? Why are you giving up without even trying?" she asked.

"I don't know what you're—"

"No. No lies, Jim. You know what and whom I'm talking about."

He stood so quickly that his chair tumbled backward. He kicked it away and leaned over the desk, turning his head to face his sister.

"What do you want me to do about it?" he shouted. "About her? About Olivia? What is there for me to do?"

Emmaline had sat back in her chair, but to her credit she did not back down. "You must tell her, Jim. You must. You must tell her you love—"

"Love? How ridiculous and addlebrained you sound, Emmaline! You sound like Nettie before she was married, constantly talking about John, and still now, even after they've been married for years. This is not about love."

"Not about love? Who sounds ridiculous now? I know you love her. Nettie and John and Mother know you love her. Adam Gentry knows you love her. It's obvious to those who know you well," she whispered.

His throat tightened and he was suddenly terrified that he would betray himself with tears or a choked cough. He walked to the bed and faced the wall, willing himself to control his breathing and emotions.

"There is nothing to be done about it, Emmaline," he said quietly. "There are too many obstacles."

"Obstacles? Our families have known each other forever, since when Daddy and Mr. Gentry first met. Mrs. Gentry could have no objections."

"But Olivia would. Miss Gentry, I mean. I have to stop thinking of her in such a familiar way."

"You've called her Olivia since you were young children. Why would you stop?"

"She'll be married someday. I'd best get some distance between us."

"Why couldn't she be married to you?"

"She is always angry with me, and I always say the wrong thing," he said. But then he thought about the day in the creek. The day she laid her hand on his bare chest and kissed him. The moment he thought of every night before closing his eyes.

"I won't badger you anymore, but I will tell you this. I think you need to have some honest discussions between the two of you. If you don't, the weight of your regrets is going to make you miserable and keep you from having any bit of happiness in your life. You are my favorite brother," she said. "I love you and want you to be happy."

* * *

HE HADN'T SEEN OLIVIA FOR MONTHS, HE'D REALIZED suddenly; she'd not been to church or into town as far as he knew. Her face was so often at the forefront of his dreams and thoughts that he hardly needed the real thing. What a whopper of a tall tale that was, he thought to himself. He wondered if he'd see her tonight, as he opened the door for his mother at the hall behind the church where the harvest dance supper was to be served. He looked around the room, and the first face he saw was Olivia Gentry's. Of course, his mother headed immediately in the direction of the Gentry table. Matt moved himself down one seat and held his former chair for Mother so she could be seated beside Eleanor Gentry. Matt seated himself again and waved a hand toward the end of the table.

"Get a chair, Somerset," he said.

"You're all going to have to move down one place on this side," Olivia said. "Mrs. Barrett and Mr. Armsworth will be joining us."

Matt groaned audibly. "Really, Livie? I would have thought his shirt collar was a little too tight to attend a town dance."

"Matt!" Annie said and looked at him wide-eyed. "He is Olivia's friend."

"He wants her money, is all," Matt said.

"It's a good thing that Mother is deep in discussion with Mrs. Somerset and didn't not hear you or she would drag you out of here by the ear," Adam said and took a long swallow of lemonade.

"I suppose it's too much to think that perhaps Mr. Armsworth is interested in me as a person, Matthew," Olivia said, her eyes focused on her food although she wasn't eating.

Jim studied her and watched as she looked up to meet her brother's eyes. She looked stricken and weary. He saw Mrs. Barrett, her nephew beside her, at the door. He cleared his throat. "There's not a man who meets you who's not interested to know more about you."

Olivia's head jerked to him just as Armsworth reached the table. Mrs. Gentry was signaling for Mrs. Barrett to join her and Mother. Armsworth put his hand on the back of the chair between Adam and Olivia.

"Is this seat taken?" he said and smiled.

"It is not. Please join us," Olivia said.

She was wearing her mask, he thought to himself, the one she donned when it was critical she remain a lady. What she really wished to do, he didn't know, although he wished he did. He wanted to know her innermost dreams, her sadness, her joy. Was she truly pleased that Armsworth had seated himself beside her?

"Armsworth. How is your work for the governor going?" Adam asked.

"Governor's office has asked me to report on the treatment of Confederate soldiers here in the western half of the state. I've been traveling to various towns and using Barrett House as my home camp," he said.

"Ex-Confederates around these parts have been generally

treated fairly, I'd say," Adam replied. "Although animosity still exists, of course."

"But the war is over," Armsworth said. "The governor wants to make sure that Confederate soldiers have all the opportunities they need to begin their lives again."

"And how will we ensure that freed slaves have the same opportunities?" Olivia asked and turned her head to look at him.

OLIVIA WATCHED HIM, WAITING, SHE SUPPOSED, FOR HIM TO shush her or treat her as a child. She could see he was carefully considering his answer. Jim was watching him, too, and glanced at her. She looked away before she felt compelled to thank him for his defense of her when Matt had said what he did. It felt like she was young again and he protected her from everything and everyone, including, on occasion, her own brothers. She could hardly blame Matt for his opinion of Armsworth, though; in some ways it was similar to her own.

"The freed Negroes would not be qualified for the opportunities I'm speaking of. They cannot read, or write, or do basic arithmetic. It would be foolish to put them in a position of government without any of those skills, both for the townspeople they were to serve and for their own interests. If they failed, as they surely would, it would only lessen opportunities for other Negroes," Armsworth said.

She disagreed but held her tongue. She had no interest in starting an argument during a meal in the church hall before the harvest dance. But she didn't have to worry. Someone else at their table had no such concerns.

"David Freeman works for me and can read and write and do numbers quicker and more accurately than me. Is he qualified to apply for these positions?" Jim asked.

"I don't see why not," Armsworth replied, wiping his fingers on his napkin.

"He's colored, Armsworth. What's your answer now?" Matt said.

Armsworth frowned and picked up a piece of fried chicken from his plate. "Weren't you in gray, Mr. Gentry?"

"I was. For a variety of reasons, including the most important one, which was that I was too young, too stupid, and too angry with my father to understand the core principles that the war addressed at the time of my enlistment. I stayed on because Gentrys are not quitters. I'd made a commitment to my superiors and to my men, and I honored that."

Annie stood abruptly, and the men followed. "The dessert table has all kinds of goodies, and I wonder if anyone's tried my Tyler custard pie," she said.

"She gets upset sometimes when someone talks about the war," Matt said when she'd left the table and the men were reseated.

"Understandable," Adam agreed and stood again. "I think I'll try her pie."

"I didn't mean to upset your wife, Mr. Gentry," Armsworth said as Adam followed Annie across the room.

"Annie has good reason to have ugly memories of the War between the States," Matt said.

Armsworth turned to Olivia. "My apologies to you. Perhaps I shouldn't have brought up such a topic in a social setting."

"It is still a tense time in our nation. But much of what separates us must be discussed and resolved among families and acquaintances before we are able to put the war behind us as a nation," she said. "If in fact, we ever do."

Olivia was accustomed to discussions on a wide range of topics with her family and with others, but there was something about Armsworth that made an uncomfortable subject more so. She looked past him now to Jim Somerset. He was staring at her as if trying to make his mind up about something. He'd been his usual taciturn self until he'd defended her and mentioned David

Freeman. She wondered if he'd speak another word the entire day. And then he proved her wrong.

"Will you save me a dance, Miss Gentry?"

Adam, having just returned with a full plate of desserts, looked at her. Her mother glanced her way.

"Of course, Jim," she said and added for no other reason that she could fathom other than her desire to hurt him, which was no longer fair to him or to herself, "I'll be dancing with Mr. Armsworth as I've agreed to allow him to escort me to the hall, but I imagine there'll be a dance or two for other gentlemen as well."

Jim nodded and stood and went to his mother. Everyone rose and Armsworth helped Mrs. Barrett to her feet.

"Go on now with Miss Gentry, Richard," Mrs. Barrett said. "I'll be walking over to the dance with Mrs. Gentry. This all reminds me of the yearly country fair in Yorkshire when I was a young girl. Everyone mixes with everyone, it seems," she said with a laugh.

Armsworth patted his aunt's shoulders and helped her place her shawl. Olivia laid her hand in Armsworth's as he escorted her to the dance.

Matt watched them walk away as Annie approached.

"My pie's all gone," she said with a smile. "Mrs. Carter asked me for the recipe."

"Why is Livie such a brat to Jim Somerset?" he said to no one particular.

Adam raised his brows and said nothing. Annie stared at him.

"Well, she loves him, that's why," she said.

"Loves who?" Matt asked.

"Olivia. She loves Jim Somerset."

"What are you talking about?" Matt asked.

Eleanor Gentry leaned close as she pulled on her gloves. "Lower your voices, please."

"Did you hear what Annie said, Mother?" Matt asked.

"Yes. Yes, I did."

"What a fool thing—"

"We're not going to discuss this topic any longer. Olivia knows her own heart," she said and turned away.

Matt watched her go. "Olivia and Jim?"

"Open your eyes, Matt. You're so busy looking at your wife you don't see anything else going on," Adam said.

"She's loved him forever, not just recently," Annie said.

"Well, damn it all to hell. You think somebody would have told me," Matt said.

CHAPTER 7

Olivia danced with Armsworth, and he proved again to be a pleasant companion. They danced the first dance, a vigorous polka, and went to find refreshments. She sipped lemonade while a gentleman poured whiskey from a flask into Armsworth's glass, the second he'd had so far that evening. He had left her for a moment to speak to his friend, Mr. Armond, and she was relieved when he did not bring Armond around to speak to her. At the end of the third dance, Jasper Englebright, Winchester's only attorney, asked her to dance, but Armsworth spoke first.

"Miss Gentry and I have just agreed to take a turn outside in the cool air," he said to Englebright. "Next dance maybe."

"A turn outside?" she said uncertainly when Mr. Englebright left them.

He smiled at her. "Please forgive me. I've been thinking about you for three months. I cannot bear to part with you just yet."

"How ridiculous you are!" she said and looked up at him with a smile. He was not smiling back. In fact, he was looking murderous. He smiled then suddenly, but Olivia's stomach was still in a knot. Had what she'd meant as a tease been taken seriously by him? Why did she feel that the more time she spent with Richard Armsworth, the less she knew him?

"Let's just walk out into the fresh air, my dear. It is stifling here," he said and ran a finger under his collar.

"The fresh air will feel good," she said and laid her arm on his.

There were other couples walking in the grassy area between the church and the meeting hall that had been cleared of its furniture for dancing. Armsworth led her out one of the open side doors. It was nearly dark outside but lanterns had been hung in trees and on poles. Couples and families escaping the heat or taking a moment from the dancing were mingling. He led her slowly through the crowd, toward the back of the main street, where soon they were very alone.

"Ah," she said and stopped and looked up to the starlit sky. "It is lovely and cool."

"It *is* lovely," he said and stepped close to her. He gathered her hands in his and leaned forward and touched his lips to hers.

Olivia concentrated on relaxing and letting the moment just be. Allowing herself to feel what it was like to be close to this man, to have a taste of some future intimacies. But there was no spark of passion on her side, no image of some yet to be reached plateau even as he pushed tightly against her and ran his tongue over the seam of her lips. She broke the kiss.

He kissed her forehead. "And what will we plan for our future, my dear?"

She stepped back in order to see his face. "Our future? I'm not sure our future includes anything past this evening for now, sir."

He tilted his head. "Nothing past this evening? Surely you don't misunderstand my intentions?"

"Any intentions you may have have not been shared with me or with my family."

Armsworth put his hands around her upper arms and closed on them. "Don't be a tease, Olivia. My intent has always been to make you my bride. I may have been high-handed to some degree, but I have allowed some girlish sentimentality over these perceived slights. I have apologized. That is behind us now."

Olivia arched her brows. "Perceived slights? That is your interpretation of past events between us?"

Armsworth frowned. "Never mind. I can see that I've upset you."

She wasn't upset. She was furious. "Please release me."

But he didn't. He pulled her tightly against him and ran his hand down to her bottom. "Quit fidgeting. This marriage will be advantageous to us both."

"No," she said and shook her head, pulling her mouth from his. "No. Let me go."

But he held her tightly and had backed her up against the darkened boards on the back of the telegraph office. She was thinking she'd have to shout for help. She didn't want to. She didn't want to be in the middle of another public drama. But she was starting to panic even with hundreds of neighbors nearby who would help her if necessary. Her heart was pounding in her chest, fast and hard, and she heard each beat as a boom in her ear. A lantern lit near her, blinding her and making her unable to see who was holding it.

"Miss Gentry," Louis Armond said. "This is such a public setting for such a passionate embrace. What would your neighbors think?"

"There was no need for this, Armond," Armsworth said and shielded his eyes with one hand. "Put the lantern down. I can't see."

Olivia pushed with all of her might against Armsworth when he let go of her arm to cover his eyes. She barely slipped past him, feeling the touch of his hand on the shoulder of her dress. If he came after her now, she would scream. She would scream at the top of her lungs. She could see lanterns swinging in the breeze and people milling about straight ahead. They would help her. She tried to calm her breathing even as she hurried.

JIM SAW HER COMING ACROSS THE OPEN GRASS PAST WHERE folks were standing together in small groups, drinking or just talking and laughing. He could tell there was something wrong with her as she walked up to him, a false smile on her face, her hands visibly shaking. He looked over her shoulder to where she came from but didn't see anyone. She almost walked directly into him even though she was looking right at him.

"Oh," she said as if she'd just noticed him. "This is our dance, isn't it?"

"What is the matter?" he asked.

"What do you mean? Has someone said something to you?"

"No. What is the matter?"

She shook her head as tears came to her eyes. "Please," she whispered. "Please. Just dance with me."

She took his arm when he held it out and walked her into the hall as the musicians were starting. He put a hand at her waist and waited until she put her hand on his shoulder so he could lead her onto the floor. Others were twirling by but he chose a half-tempo rhythm much like many of the older couples near them. He was worried she'd stumble or even fall. He'd never seen her look so fragile, and frightened even, in all the time he'd known her. She looked up at him with wide eyes and trembling lips. He wasn't sure if he could continue dancing, as he'd far prefer to pick her up and carry her away from here or from whatever troubled her.

"You must tell me," he said finally when he could no longer be silent. "Has someone hurt you? What has happened? Shall I take you to Matt or Adam?"

Her face reddened and she shook her head. But her eyes stopped and widened at something over his shoulder. He looked back and saw Richard Armsworth staring at her.

"Do not bow your head. Look up at me and smile even though it's not what you wish to do," he said softly.

She responded to him with a tentative smile, her hand quivering against his palm. She was a singularly beautiful woman. She was dressed in a gown the color of honey, accentuating her dark red hair and matching the pale freckles across her nose. It was then he noticed a tear in the fabric of her dress, a few threads sticking out at odd angles, at the corner of her squared neckline. She looked down to where he was looking and peered up at him with panicked eyes. He danced her right out of the large, open double doors at the back of the hall, and to the deserted side of the building.

"Why is your dress torn? What has happened?"

"Nothing . . . I can't . . . nothing." But she was gulping for breath and did not finish her words.

"Armsworth? It's Armsworth, isn't it. Has he hurt you?"

She grabbed his forearms. "Don't do anything. Please."

His skin itched with the desire to do violence. His heart was beating hard in his ears and his fists were clenched. But she was pleading with him, and he didn't have the heart to deny her anything, especially when she was in such a state.

She took a few deep breaths and closed her eyes. "He kissed me. I let him, but he didn't stop when I asked him to, and then Mr. Armond was there with a lantern and my dress must have torn as I pulled away. Armsworth told me we were going to marry and that I knew and understood that from the beginning."

And then she crumbled into his arms, weeping. He held her to him while she cried, soaking his shirt while he petted her hair and told her softly to hush. That he was there holding her and that no one would get past him to harm her.

She stopped then, wiping her face on his handkerchief and taking deep breaths. "I'm fine. Would you take me to my mother? I've panicked for no reason. None at all."

"Will you tell your mother what happened? Your brothers? They should know."

"Please say nothing. I beg of you," Olivia said and looked at him with pleading eyes.

"I won't say anything for now, but that doesn't mean I may not kill him."

She looked up sharply, took his arm, and walked back into the hall, unhurriedly. He found Mrs. Gentry with his own mother and some other women from town. He released Olivia's arm and leaned close to her.

"I won't tell Adam unless I hear that Armsworth has visited Paradise or that he has bothered you in some other way."

"Please . . ."

Jim shook his head. "If it were one of my sisters, I would want to know. I would need to know."

She nodded and turned to her mother. Jim wound his way through the crowd until he was in sight of Richard Armsworth. He would stay on the man's tail and let him know he had best stay clear of Olivia Gentry without ever speaking a word to the man.

* * *

"WHAT'S THIS ABOUT YOU AND MY SISTER?" MATT GENTRY asked from where he sat on the bank of the creek near the dammed-up area that they had swum in earlier that summer.

Jim pulled a worm from a tin can and threaded it on his hook. He shrugged. "Don't know what you're talking about."

"Ha!" Matt said and barked a laugh. "I said the same thing, then Annie and Adam confirmed it, and even my mother implied it. Adam said I was too busy looking at my wife to notice anything, and I think he might be right."

Jim dropped his fishing line in the fast-moving water and said nothing.

"If you won't even talk about it, you must have it bad."

"Do you really want me to say something about your sister?"

"Well, hell, no, nothing like that!" Matt said and shuddered and then turned his face to him. "But you care for her, don't you?"

"I have the utmost respect for your sister. She's a lady."

He didn't want to look at his friend Matt. He was afraid his feelings would be written all over his face and that Matt would be unable to be silent about them once he understood. But he did finally glance at him. Matt was staring at him with narrowed eyes.

"I had my first woman somewhere outside of Spotsylvania shortly after I'd been ordered to take my men to join the Army of the Trans-Mississippi. Maybe eight or so months after I'd left home. I thought then that I'd like to brag about it to you, even knowing I barely got the clothes off that girl and my buttons undone before I'd disgraced myself. I was certain you were as much a virgin as I when I left Winchester, but you were here and I spent the next few years climbing in and out of beds from Dallas to Lexington. I was an embarrassment to myself and my family."

Jim stretched a leg out in front of him and poked a stone with the heel of his boot. He stared gloomily across the water. He didn't want to hear Matt's confessions or think of anything untoward as it inevitably led to thoughts of Olivia.

"Is that why you asked me to come fishing? So you could confess some old indiscretions? I'd rather not hear about them," Jim said. "Do you think we'll have a hard winter? The almanac is saying not."

"Do you ever go over to Romney or Middletown?"

He shrugged. "Why would I go there?"

"Because you don't diddle with a woman in your own town. Didn't your father ever tell you that?"

Jim shook his head.

"You never spent a night away and told your family you were looking at something for the forge or some other made-up story?"

He went to stand but Matt held his shoulder.

"My God, Jim! Are you saying you've slept with someone right here in town? June? Not June from over at the saloon. Dear Lord! She's got to be fifty if she's a day!"

"No! June? No!"

"Well, who else then? Is there a widow about that I don't know about?"

"I'm not talking about this to you." Jim stood up, pulled his line out of the water, and dumped the worms remaining in his can near the creek bank. "I've never been interested in a widow or a woman like June."

"You're not like the Romans, are you?" Matt said as he looked up.

"No, Matt. I'm as interested in women as much as you are. I just don't think . . . it's not right somehow . . . doing that with whoever . . . she'll be special."

"So, you've not . . ."

Jim glared at him, willing him to shut up. Matt jumped to his feet.

"But somebody's got to know one end of the thing from the other! You'll be marrying a virgin. Who's to say what to do if you've not done it before!"

Jim shook his head and laughed. "You're lucky you married Annie, because she may be the only thing that keeps you from being a complete idiot. Humans have been procreating for thousands of years and so far nobody's looked about on their wedding night and said, 'What do I do now?' I imagine my bride and I, if I am so fortunate to marry, will figure things out in our own way with no prior instruction or demonstrations."

Matt grinned and then laughed. "Can you see it? Can you see it in your head? Jeremiah Finch hollering from the second-story window of the hotel on his wedding night asking what goes where?"

Jim laughed again, thinking about the skinny young man who worked for the postmaster, always reading a book and bumping into walls. "I imagine he's got the same parts as you and me. Even he'd figure it out."

He picked up his fishing pole and walked to where his horse was tied to a tree and quietly chewing on a shrub. He mounted and fit the pole in his saddlebag. Matt pulled the reins from the tree and handed them to him.

"So, you're not going to take a ride over to Romney or Middletown," Matt said.

Jim took the reins and put his hat on his head. He looked down at his friend and touched his knees to his horse. He wasn't about to say out loud to his oldest friend or to anyone really that he had never had a woman.

There were a few times he'd been close over the years, once with a young woman who served meals at the hotel. She'd made her availability known to him subtly and then more overtly when he didn't respond to her shy comments. Finally, she told him to meet her at her house just outside of town where she lived with her invalid grandmother and young brother. She'd pulled him inside the cabin when he arrived, pushing his shirt from his shoulders and telling him her brother was out in the woods and her grandmother was deaf and asleep. He followed her behind a curtain to a small metal bed. She'd pulled her dress over her head and stood before him naked. She'd waited as he stared, until she finally picked up his hand from his side and placed it on her breast. She'd shivered and closed her eyes.

He was tempted. Oh, he was tempted. But in the end, or rather before anything had really started, even with a pulsing, erect cock, he couldn't do it. He didn't know her. He just didn't think he could join himself to her and walk away. And a quick glance around the room confirmed that he wouldn't stay. He'd picked up her dress and handed it to her and apologized. He told her he loved another and couldn't betray that woman. The woman in his heart. The girl had teared up at the same time as they both heard a young boy's voice calling her name. He pulled his shirt over his shoulders and slipped out the door before the brother saw him.

He took her a basket of food a few times a year after that and dropped off clothing his sisters and brother had outgrown. She married a local dairy farmer a few years back, and when he saw them in town together on occasion, he always tipped his hat to her and spoke to her as if they were old friends. She was clearly happy with her husband, who'd moved her, her grandmother, and her brother to his farm. What would those meetings have been like if he'd put her under him on that metal bed and used her body to satisfy his urgings? He could hardly bear the thought of it.

CHAPTER 8

Olivia wiped her face with the linen towel she'd tucked into her apron strings. The Gentry household was finishing the last of the canning for the season. Today was her favorite day of all since she was a young girl, even knowing it would be a long, hot day making jar after jar of apple butter. Mabel and Eleanor were in charge of the stoves, while Annie, Olivia, Beatrice, and Jenny cleaned and cored bushels of apples. The kitchen smelled wonderful, certainly better than the last two days when they'd put up pickles and beets, and the women talked about every imaginable subject, making the day go faster. Teddy had just woken from his nap in the cradle Matt had carried in, and Annie picked him up and took him out of the hot kitchen to feed him.

"Go now," Eleanor Gentry said to Mabel. "You're exhausted and were up half the night after hearing the news about your brother. Beatrice and Jenny can be excused, too, to do a quick cleanup of the bedrooms. There is little left to do, and Olivia and I can manage."

"Thank you so much," Mabel said as she pulled her apron over her head. "I'm near ready to fall asleep on my feet."

"We've all worked very hard this week. Beatrice, when you and

Jenny are done upstairs heat water for Mabel to bathe. Olivia and I will need a bath, too. Tomorrow, you may both work a few hours in the morning and then the rest of the day is yours. You've all done a very good job. I thank you."

Jenny and Beatrice thanked Eleanor and hurried out of the kitchen, chattering about what they would do and where they would go tomorrow afternoon. Olivia dumped the last of the apple skins and cores into two buckets that she sat near the open door. Eleanor dipped the apple butter into the few remaining mismatched jars and poured the end of the melted paraffin on top.

"I'm out of wax. We'll have to eat these last two jars up now instead of putting them in the cellar."

"That is fine with me. I'm hungry for some of Mabel's biscuits and this apple butter. It smells delicious and makes the whole house smell good, as it has for as long as I can remember," Olivia said.

"You always liked this day, even when you were a little girl. I used to have to chase you down to help with the pickling but not when we make applesauce or apple butter. Someday, you'll have a little girl to help you in your kitchen when you're putting up."

Olivia walked away from the long, planked work table of the summer kitchen to an open window. She propped her elbows on the sill and looked out toward the house. She could see Jenny filling buckets of water at the pump at the sink. She didn't want to think about a child of her own. She didn't want to think about what was required of her to get that child. Like courtship and marriage and intimacy.

Her plans to marry with a purpose had not worked out in reality as they had in her head. In her ridiculous daydreams. How could she have been so naïve? She'd been thinking that she might have been at the beginning of a satisfying courtship where like minds and compatible persons could forge a life together based on respect and similar goals. She was even willing to forgive

Armsworth for his earlier missteps, believing that two people would need time to adjust and understand each other.

Armsworth, however, *had* planned a marriage with a purpose of his own. His own satisfaction and goals. She wasn't silly enough to believe he'd fallen in love with her. More likely he'd planned his campaign, brief as it was, long before ever meeting her. She was a prize to him, perhaps able to impress the governor with her connections, and he felt no compunction to honor or even notice her true feelings or gauge her regard for him. He wasn't intent upon or even interested in understanding her. Why had she continued thinking he might? Why had she invited him to sit with her at the meal before the dance? She had already been skeptical of his worthiness at that time, and his behavior only confirmed her worst fears about him that night.

What am I about?

"Olivia?"

She turned to her mother.

"I've been talking to you for these last five minutes and you haven't answered me once."

"I'm sorry, Mother. I must have been lost in thought. I'll take these apple skins to the barns and see if George would like to give them to the foals, although he must have too many pails already since Beatrice and Jenny have carried so many out already."

"Put the buckets down, dear. Won't you sit down with me and have a cup of coffee? I've just fixed myself some."

Olivia obediently sat the apple skins and cores by the door. She sat down at the table without looking up and took a sip of the coffee her mother had fixed her. She looked up when Eleanor squeezed her hand.

"You have been upset since the dance, Olivia. Did something happen between you and Mr. Armsworth?"

Olivia could feel the rise of heat up her neck, even more so than the warm kitchen accounted for. She'd always been close to her mother, but it had been quite a while since she'd said much of anything to her past the normal conversations of living in the same house. She looked up at her but saw only a blurry image through her tears.

"Sometimes I don't understand myself," she said finally after wiping her eyes.

"What don't you understand?"

"What I want for myself."

She sipped her coffee and glanced at her mother. The woman that had been, and continued to be, the rock and the solid ground that the Gentry family was built on. Olivia loved her with every ounce of herself and missed her father desperately. The thought of him brought an ache to her chest that didn't seem to lessen with time. Why had she closed herself off from her mother's wisdom and love?

"I guess it began with Mr. Dunderage," she said finally and looked up. "How did I not know what he was about? How was I so blind? I'm not stupid, Mother. You've given me an education many young women only dream about. I've studied Latin and philosophies and astronomy and classic literature even above the lessons you and Daddy taught us here at home. How was it that I was unable to discern Mr. Dunderage's intentions were not honorable?"

Eleanor shook her head. "Olivia! You are still concerned about him?"

"No! I'm not concerned about him at all. I'm concerned about myself. Apparently, I've learned nothing from that experience, contrary to what I've stated adamantly."

"Listen to me," Eleanor said and waited until she looked up. "You are equating your intelligence and your knowledge with your emotions. They are distinctly separate."

"Even if they are separate, I am able to look back at Mr. Dunderage's actions and know that he was insincere."

"Of course, you can now. Your emotions aren't engaged. We're always able to see things rationally when our emotions aren't involved."

"I suppose."

"Has it been the same with Mr. Armsworth?"

Olivia nodded. "He is handsome and charming, but he isn't interested in *me*. He is interested in marriage but not with me as a person. It's humiliating to find myself in this predicament again. I should have never asked him to join us at the church dance."

"Olivia, darling! You are much too hard on yourself! Nothing so horrible has happened, has it? You have been in his company a few times and determined that he isn't worthy of your regard. That's all."

"That's all, isn't it?" Olivia asked, although her lip trembled. "I've made myself miserable. I cannot blame that on Mr. Armsworth, can I?"

"Let me tell you something I've never shared with you before. You are an adult woman now and perhaps you will learn something from your mother's mistakes." She held up her hands in protest when Olivia began to speak. "I was a young, impressionable woman once, too, although it was a very long time ago. Did you know I was engaged to be married when our family set out from Allentown to go to my father's new church?"

Olivia shook her head. "To Daddy?"

"No. I was engaged to a young minister who was planning on joining our procession to western Virginia and help my father fulfill his dream of starting a church there. His name was William Dodgekins."

Eleanor stood and leaned against the stove behind her. She stared out the window for a few moments, remembering, Olivia imagined, those horrible days after her family, Olivia's grandparents and aunts, were murdered.

"I escaped that night," Eleanor said and looked at her. "I've told you some of this, and I'm sure you've heard bits and pieces of the rest. I escaped in my nightgown and coat. I could hear my mother's screams and gunshots. I knew they were all dead and I was terrified the men were after me. I kept running in the direction of Winchester, at least what I thought was the direction, but didn't arrive in town until the next morning. I went directly to the church to find William."

"He was to stay and finish his ministerial education with Reverend Buckland within the month and then he would join us at our new church. I'd corresponded with William for close to a year at that point and was very satisfied with how my life would continue on when I left my mother and father. I would marry William and be a minister's wife just as my mother had done.

"When I found William that morning, I was completely hysterical and still terrified that someone had followed me." She looked up at Olivia and smiled softly. "William was most concerned that I'd appeared in town in my nightgown and that my hair was not pinned up."

"He was concerned about your clothing? Your mother and father and my aunts had just been murdered," Olivia whispered and swallowed. "What could he have been thinking?"

"Ah," Eleanor replied. "There is the crux of the story. He was not thinking of me. He was thinking of appearances and his own self-worth. He was a self-righteous ass."

Olivia's eyes rounded and she smiled slowly. "Mother. I have never once known you to say such a word."

Eleanor chuckled. "If there is anyone who deserves it more, I do not know."

"What happened then?"

"I wanted William to come with me back to our wagon and help me bury my family and say the prayers. He wouldn't go with me. He said it would have been unseemly for us to travel to the wagon without a chaperone as we were not married. I think he was afraid the bandits were still there. Ultimately, he was right."

"Unseemly? What a silly notion to be concerned about in that situation."

"Yes. And then I made the dreadful mistake of going myself. I had no shovel or anything to properly bury them with, but I went anyway. I was not quite in my right mind at the time. I was crying, sobbing really, when I actually saw all their dead bodies and had climbed into the wagon just to touch my mother's shawl and that's when a horrible man found me and stole me away. Eleven days I was with him. Eleven long days. I was lucky to live and to hang on to my virtue until your father rescued me."

Olivia wondered if she would have the wherewithal and the courage to survive what her mother had. She'd not been tested in that way, and she thanked the dear Lord that she hadn't been. Was she being petty by continuing to dwell on what was to come in her life? After all, Mr. Armsworth had done her no real harm, had he? He had scared her certainly and acted disrespectfully, but she'd been able to get away from him.

"Did you ever see him again? Mr. Dodgekins, that is?"

"I did. After your father killed all of the bandits and I was able to travel, he brought me back to Winchester. I went directly to the church after leaving your father and found William there. He told me that he wanted nothing to do with me. That I was no longer fit to be his wife," Eleanor said and continued in a whisper. "I told him I had no one. That I was completely alone. I begged him to reconsider since we'd corresponded for so long."

"How horrible!" Olivia said.

Eleanor nodded, looking across the room, lost in thought. She turned back to Olivia with a wry smile. "That is when your father arrived and punched him in the nose. It was glorious!"

Olivia laughed.

"Beauregard had followed me and listened to our conversation. He punched him in the stomach several times, too, before William dropped to his knees. Your father held his bloody face in his hands and told him he was going straight to hell. Then he turned to me and told me he would take me to wherever I needed to go. I didn't realize it then, but that moment was when I fell in love with him."

"Oh, Daddy," Olivia said as tears sprang in her eyes and she looked up at her mother. "I miss him terribly, but you must miss him so much more."

"I do, darling. I miss him desperately," she said as she sat down beside her. "He told me many years ago that he would love me into the evermore and I believed him then and I believe he loves me still. I believe his love for us all is quite real."

"I have been a ninny, I think," Olivia said and stood to refill their cups. "I had decided to marry and was trying to be practical about it. But there is nothing practical about it at all, is there?"

Eleanor shook her head. "No. There is not. The point of me telling you this story, though, is that I thought William Dodgekins was my whole world. Sometimes it takes time to sort out our feelings, and sometimes we see how others act and know then that they are not who we thought or dreamed they were. We must be courageous enough to walk away from our dreams sometimes."

"I hate the idea, I just hate it . . . that I may never . . . fall in love. If I decide to wait for love I may be too old for children or unwilling to change my life so drastically. I always thought I'd marry someday."

Eleanor stood, gathered her recipe book and her apron from the table before walking to the door. "I'm going to wash myself and read a book, I think. It's been a long week." She stopped at the door and turned. She stared at Olivia and smiled. "Are you quite certain you are not already in love?"

"No, Mother. I'm not in love with Mr. Armsworth."

Eleanor tilted her head and smiled softly. "I never thought you were in love with Armsworth, dear."

She watched her mother walk out the door. *Who else could I possibly be in love with?* She swallowed and hurried from the summer kitchen, hurried away from the face from her dreams.

* * *

JIM SOMERSET STOOD IN THE ENTRANCE OF THE MERCANTILE, his hand on the knob of the door. She was standing there, her back to him, and he couldn't drag his eyes from her hair, loosely pulled up with a few strands escaping to the long white column of her neck. It was as though he'd just run his hands in those tresses starting to tumble from their confines. The red, brown, and gold highlights were sparkling in the sunlight coming through the window as she laughed at something Marabelle said. He closed the door and walked to the counter.

"Hello, Marabelle," he said.

"Oh, hello, Jim. You're probably here for the items you ordered. They're in the back. I'll get them now."

He watched Marabelle walk toward the door where he could see shelves and stacks of inventory. She stopped and talked to a young child looking at the candy in the glass jars on the counter.

Olivia turned to him, and he swallowed and turned his hat in his hand. It was painful seeing her. He'd decided his heart couldn't take it any longer and hadn't been out in public much at all over the last month or so, even to church, willing to bear his mother's wrath for those missed services. But here she was before him in a moss-colored wool coat that matched her eyes. She was beautiful. He stared at her, feeling as if he was falling, falling into the green depths of her eyes.

"Hello, Jim," she said and looked up at him.

"H-hello."

He'd dreamed of seeing her, talking to her, waiting for her to smile at him, but none of the interesting conversation he'd spoken in his dream state was coming to mind. Maybe he was going to have to move away. He didn't think he could live his life out and still cling to his dignity if he was tongue-tied every time he saw her and relived the meeting for days and weeks afterwards. Maybe he *was* going to have to move to another town. Then she smiled up at him, and his sanity slipped away.

"You've shaved your beard some. I don't know if I recall ever seeing your cheeks before," she said.

Her eyes were gay and mischievous, and he thought he might die just to have her look at him thus. He'd gotten worse, he could tell. Before the harvest dinner, he'd been able to control his feelings about her, but now he was unable to be rational about the emotions she summoned in him. He loved her. He loved everything about her. He wanted her far beyond normal male urgings when seeing a beautiful and desirable woman. Her smile was fading as he continued to stare at her silently, still turning his hat.

"Well," she said. "Tell your mother and sisters I said hello. I'll be going now."

She walked past him, and he heard the tinkle of the bell above the door as she opened it. He looked up to see Marabelle staring at him and shaking her head. It was pity in her eyes, he could see. He was pitiful. He turned and hurried to the door, leaving everything on the counter that he'd come to pick up.

"Olivia," he said as he opened the door.

"Yes, Jim?" she said when she turned.

He could swear there was hope in her eyes even though she wasn't smiling. She was looking up at him, and he watched her swallow.

"Have you," he began and cleared his throat. "Have you had your noonday meal?"

She shook her head. "No, I haven't. I've just done some ordering with Marabelle and was going back to Paradise."

Jim nodded. "Well, then, I'll let you go on your way."

They stood a few feet apart, she holding her little beaded bag at her waist, and he twirling his hat. She looked down at her leather-gloved hands and then out to the street where buggies were passing. She finally looked at him.

"Why did you ask me if I'd had my noonday meal?"

"I was going over to Martha's. I thought maybe you'd like to join me," he said and held his breath.

Her smile was slow and breathtaking to behold. It was as if every scrap of joy he'd ever felt burst in his chest at the sight of that smile.

"I'd like that, Jim. Very much," she said and grinned.

He held out his arm, hoping she couldn't see his tremors, and escorted her across the busy street to Martha's. He opened the door for her to enter, and every patron turned toward them. He wanted to beat on his chest and howl at the moon. This woman chose him, he thought with triumph. At least for an hour or so, she had. He hung her coat and his on the hooks by the door and rubbed his hands together to get the coldness out of them, whether because he was nervous or because the November weather had turned decidedly chilly.

Martha walked over to their table. "I have beef stew with biscuits or cold ham on bread with chowchow or anything on the menu. There's stewed apples for dessert."

They ordered their meals, and Martha brought him coffee and Olivia warmed chocolate. She wrapped her hands around the mug and looked up at him. He couldn't stop staring at her as she gazed about the room, her eyes coming to rest on his every now and again, before looking away or at her hands. He wasn't uncomfortable with the silence between them, although he wondered if she was.

"You can see them now," he said finally.

OLIVIA LOOKED AT JIM ACROSS THE TABLE FROM HER. SHE thought she'd die in the mercantile, just shrivel up and drop to the floor, when he didn't speak to her. But she didn't have any idea what he was talking about now.

"See what?" she said.

"My cheeks."

"Oh, yes," she said and smiled. "You've always worn your beard very thick, and you've trimmed it up some. It looks well on you."

He nodded and sipped his coffee while staring at her over the rim of his cup.

"How is Emmaline? She didn't attend the last Ladies Hospital Aid and Recovery meeting at Barrett House. Your mother said she was under the weather."

"She's fine."

"That's good to hear," she said and folded her hands in her lap. She wondered if he talked much to Matt when they were together. She'd ask her brother but then she'd have to listen to his teases.

Jim cleared his throat. "She, um, she wasn't sick."

"Oh?"

Jim shook his head.

"Emmaline hates those meetings. I'm not surprised she didn't want to go," Olivia said.

Their food arrived, and she watched him snap open his napkin and place it on his lap. He waited for her to begin and then took small bites, chewing slowly with all the decorum Eleanor Gentry would have expected at her table. To this day her mother chided Matt on his manners, but she would have nothing to say about Jim Somerset's. It struck her then that he reminded her of Adam. Controlled and gentlemanly and aware of the proprieties.

"You're right—she didn't want to go. Was Mr. Armsworth at Barrett House during your meeting?" he asked as he slathered butter on his biscuit without looking at her.

She watched him spread the butter from one side of the biscuit to the other and back again as if it hadn't worked correctly the first time he'd done it. He finally stopped and placed his knife on the table. He was waiting for her answer.

"No. He wasn't there," she said. His eyes met hers. "I'm not privy to or interested in his schedule."

He took a bite of his stew, a very small grin visible. "I'm glad to hear that."

She couldn't stop a blush from climbing her cheeks. She applied herself to her meal and risked a look at him occasionally, only to find him looking at her and quickly looking back down to his plate.

"We're having a dinner for a friend of Adam's and his sister on Saturday evening. They are arriving by train from Washington and will be staying with us for a few days. We'll just be having cards and a game or two after dinner unless we can persuade Aunt Brigid to play the piano for us," Olivia said.

Jim wiped his mouth with his napkin and raised his brows. "Adam's friend?"

"A friend from Franklin College in Pennsylvania, which he attended before the war broke out. Darien Wright is his name, and his sister is Josephine."

"Ah."

"Well?"

"Well, what?"

"Will you come? To dinner, that is?" She knew her face was hot. Perhaps she shouldn't have been so forward. Perhaps he would think she was still the immature younger sister. She should have never said anything and had Mother invite him and Mrs. Somerset together.

"Yes," he said. "I will use my best manners and try not to embarrass you or your brothers."

She took a deep breath and smiled. "Embarrass Matt? I don't believe that's possible!"

CHAPTER 9

"There'll be eight of us for dinner on Saturday. Mabel is going to roast a turkey or pheasants depending on what Ben sees when he's in the woods. Perhaps you can choose some wines from the cellar, Adam," Eleanor Gentry said as they gathered at Paradise for Sunday dinner after church. "I won't have much in the way of flowers, but we've dried some from the summer and I think I'll be able to make a credible arrangement."

"I'll check this week on the wine, Mother," Adam said. "But don't put yourself out too much. Darien is an old friend and wouldn't want us to go to any trouble on his account."

"They'll be guests of Paradise, Adam. We're going to make sure their stay is comfortable. And anyway, I understand Miss Wright is quite the Washington socialite and is influential on a number of causes I'm interested in."

"We don't want this paragon to think we're nothing but back-woods horse traders," Matt said with a laugh. "You better wear a nice dress on Saturday, Annie, or Mother will have your hide."

Eleanor laid her fork and knife down beside her plate. "Annie is a grown woman with good manners and is well-equipped to dress appropriately for the occasion." She turned her head to her daughter-in-law, who was grinning. "I'm sorry to talk about you as if you aren't here, dear, but your husband was being rude and I won't tolerate it."

"Yes, ma'am," Annie said and smiled at her husband. "I do enjoy when your ma puts you in your place."

"There'll be Mother, me, Matt, Annie, Olivia, Aunt Brigid, and the two Wrights," Adam said. "We'll need three bottles for dinner, and I'll bring up some port for the gentlemen."

"Actually, there'll be nine," Olivia said. She willed herself not to blush and concentrated on cutting the meat on her plate.

Adam repeated the names and counted on his fingers as he did. "Eight."

"I've asked Jim Somerset to join us for dinner," she said. "You don't mind, do you Mother?"

"Somerset? Where'd you see him, Livie? He hasn't shown his face around town for a month. And why would you invite him anyway?" Matt asked.

"Matthew?" Aunt Brigid said and pointed with her fork. "You've got gravy all over your chin, boy."

"Of course, you are welcome to invite Jim," her mother said. "He's nearly family, and I haven't seen him for an age."

"Where did you see him, Livie?" Matt asked as he wiped his face with a napkin and shot a look to his aunt.

Olivia dabbed her mouth. She must be careful to appear casual in her reply or her mother would pepper her with a hundred questions and Matt would tease her endlessly. "I saw him at the mercantile, and we had our noon meal together. I asked him then. It seemed the polite thing to do."

"It was the polite thing to do," her mother said. "We will have nine for dinner on Saturday."

"I'll get another bottle out of the cellar," Adam said and winked at her.

Olivia finished adding cream-colored trim to the hem of the navy velvet dress she was planning on wearing that evening. She heard a commotion below, Matt talking, and an unknown voice reply.

"Mother! Livie!" Matt called out.

Olivia straightened her skirts as she stood, pulled the door of her sitting room closed and hurried down the steps. She saw from the first landing that Matt was standing just inside the door with a man and woman that she didn't recognize.

"Welcome! Welcome to Paradise," Eleanor said and smiled as she stepped off the last step. "Adam is so sorry he was unable to pick you up at the station."

"That's quite alright, Mrs. Gentry. Adam told me he might be out of town until the evening and to took look for his baby brother at the station," Wright said with a laugh and pointed a thumb in Matt's direction. "Baby brother? He's as big as a house!"

Eleanor laughed and turned to include the woman standing just behind Wright. "You've met my middle child, Matthew, I'm Eleanor Gentry, and this is my youngest, Olivia. You've no doubt been traveling all day. Would you like to rest in your rooms? We'll serve some tea and coffee in a half hour or so or we can bring it to your room."

"I would love a chance to change and freshen up," Josephine Wright said and smiled.

Eleanor turned to the Paradise housekeeper standing in the doorway of the main room. "Jenny, please have George send someone to carry the luggage and trunks inside."

"Let me take you to your room," Olivia said to Miss Wright.

"Thank you, Miss Gentry," she replied.

"Please don't stand on ceremony here at Paradise," Eleanor said as they began up the staircase. "I'm Eleanor, and she is Olivia."

"And I'm Josephine and my brother is Darien."

Olivia led the way down the wide, carpeted hallway on the

second floor to one of the guest rooms. She opened the door and allowed Josephine to pass.

"How beautiful," the woman said in a near whisper and turned around slowly in the middle of the room. "I feel as though I've just walked into a blooming garden."

"Mother and I redecorated these rooms a few years ago. We went to Philadelphia for the fabrics and wallcoverings. We call it the rose room."

"I can see why," she said and trailed a hand over the low dressing table. She peeked out through the sheer pale green curtains.

Olivia joined her and pointed to the wing of the house that angled away from the main part of Paradise they were in. "The window right there is your brother's room. The blue room."

"Are the two windows beyond Darien's additional bedrooms?"

"No. That is Adam's bedroom and sitting room and office with a bathing chamber and dressing room. As Adam got older, Mother felt he should have a private apartment of sorts," Olivia said and laughed. "I just think she didn't want him leaving Paradise!"

Josephine smiled and continued to stare out the window until there was a knock at the door and Jenny looked in.

"Just put them here," Jenny said to two stable hands. "I'll have Beatrice hang all your things in just a few minutes, Miss Wright. We'll be happy to draw a bath for you if you'd like."

Olivia watched both of the young men now putting the trunks on the floor of the room, while surreptitiously glancing at Josephine Wright. The dark-haired one, Andrew was his name, Olivia thought, took one last long look at her before pulling the door closed.

Josephine was discussing something about her dresses and shoes with Jenny. She was tall with yellow-blond hair underneath a wide gold fabric hat with pheasant feather adornments worn at a tilt. Jenny was helping her off with her bright purple coat, trimmed with gold braid, revealing a silk dress in the same color. Her mouth was wide, almost too wide, and rouged, although there was a hint about it of something wild or passionate that might have been the reason the young men were staring so intently at her. She had the palest blue eyes Olivia had ever seen, and her cheeks were pink either from the cold or a cosmetic. She wasn't classically beautiful, handsome was a better word, but more than that there was something about her that would make both men and women look twice. She was sophisticated and subtle and exuded a feminine charm that Olivia wished she could duplicate.

"Please let Jenny or I know if there is anything else you'll need," Olivia said and walked toward the door. "We're so happy to entertain Adam's friends."

"I'm going to rest and come down for supper, I think. Traveling makes me so weary."

"We'll have some wine in the main room at six and will eat by six thirty. Would you like some cakes or bread before you rest? Coffee? Tea?"

"Tea would be wonderful!"

"I'll see to it, Jenny, until Beatrice helps you here."

Olivia closed the door and met Darien Wright in the hallway. He was striding around the corner from Adam's wing of the house and stopped when he saw her. He smiled. Josephine was not the only attractive one in the family. He had the same pale blue eyes but his hair was not as blond as his sister's. He had an open, amiable countenance that Olivia immediately liked.

"Olivia! How gracious you and your mother are! I have a splendid large room, not fit for a lay about as myself!"

She laughed. "Adam warned me that you are a jokester, Darien."

"And Adam told me that you were the typical little sister, although my own sister does not fall into that category, by far."

"What exactly is a typical little sister?"

"Well," he said and took an exaggerated pose as if contemplating a difficult mathematical problem, "something about skinny, long arms and legs, all teeth in a face, constantly demanding his time and throwing the occasional walnut at his head."

"When I was twelve, yes," she said with a smile. "That would have described me perfectly. But as you can see, I've grown up a bit and don't *usually* lob walnuts at him any longer."

He took a quick perusal of her from her toes to the top of her head. He smiled lazily and indulgently and looked into her eyes. "You certainly have grown up."

She covered her mouth with her hand to stifle a giggle. "What an outrageous flirt you are!"

He covered his heart with his hand. "You wound me, Olivia! Allow me to sit next to you at supper, and I can take pains to change your mind about me."

"Mother has already determined the seating. I believe you are to her left and beside my sister-in-law, Annie."

"Then I will convince those two women that there is no artifice in my heart, and they will in turn convince you!"

She shook her head and smiled at him. Why couldn't she be feeling short of breath around this man? Surely, he was nothing like Richard Armsworth if he'd been Adam's friend for a decade or more. She appreciated his good humor, his compliments, and his handsome face. But appreciation didn't make her heart beat hard in her chest or make her feel breathless.

* * *

OLIVIA MET HER MOTHER, MATT, AND ANNIE IN THE MAIN room shortly before six. Matt poured her a small glass of wine and she sampled the cured meats, pickles, and cheeses that had been laid out on a side table. The room looked lovely, of course, and the last of the day's sunshine glinted through the windows, moving and bouncing with the shadows of the few leaves still attached to the tree limbs that overhung the front of the house. The fire was crackling, making the room cozy even with her arms bare near to her shoulders. The dark blue velvet gown she'd chosen had ring sleeves of cream lace with a low bodice, a small bustle, and an underskirt of cream-colored satin.

Her mother was in her best finery, and Annie lovely in pale green.

"Are you going to church on your way home from dinner?" she whispered to Matt as she stood beside him.

He looked at her strangely. "Church?"

"I've not seen you in a suit for some time," she said softly and smiled. "I thought perhaps you'd worn it so you could stop and chat with the reverend."

He pinched the back of her arm, making her jump and stifle a cry just as Aunt Brigid was being brought into the room in her wheeled chair.

"Aunt Brigid," he said. "Would you like to sit in the settee here by the fire? I'll help you out of your chair if you do."

"Yes, I'd like that. Turn the chair a bit so I can see everyone in the room."

Matt did as he was told, and Olivia draped a lap robe over her aunt's knees when she was settled into her seat. "Are you comfortable?"

"Yes, dear. When is your guest arriving?".

"I don't know. I imagine soon," she said. At that moment Jenny opened the door to the main room, and Jim Somerset stood in the doorway.

Her stomach flopped, her face flushed, and she licked her lips.

HE KNEW HE WAS STARING AT HER, KNEW HE SHOULD BE moving forward, stepping into the room, but his feet weren't obeying. He stood rooted to the spot in the doorway and could feel the Paradise housekeeper peering up at him. Olivia was so lovely, he just couldn't take his eyes off of her. Her hair flashed red and gold in the soft light of the room. She was wearing a blue dress that made the flawless skin of her face glow pink. The dress was low-cut like the one she wore the night he'd danced with her, and he let his eyes drift to the tops of her bosom and back to her face. He heard someone clear their throat and thought it may be Matt. He stepped into the room, and the door closed behind him. His feet wanted to go directly to her, to tower over her, to be close enough to catch the scent of roses he associated with her. He caught himself and turned toward her mother.

"Mrs. Gentry. Thank you having me."

"Of course, Jim. We're delighted you came. How is Mrs. Somerset?"

"Well, ma'am. Mother is very well and has been planning a holiday get-together," he said as his eyes drifted back to Olivia. He looked back at Mrs. Gentry, who was smiling at him and glancing at her daughter.

"When's the last time both of us were trussed up like this, Jim? It's been an age," Matt said and slapped him on the shoulder.

"Darien. Josephine. Please come in and join us," Eleanor Gentry said to the two strangers now standing in the doorway. "You've met the family, except Aunt Brigid, my father's sister who resides with us."

"What a pleasure to meet you," Darien said. "May I call you Aunt Brigid? I'm a longtime friend of your nephew, that rascal Adam."

Brigid harrumphed with a smile. "What a smooth talker you are! Of course, you may call me Aunt Brigid. And who is the lovely young lady?"

"My sister. Josephine Wright."

Matt leaned close to Jim while staring at Josephine. "She's the kind of woman that makes a man think about cold nights and warm sheets," he said quietly.

Jim nodded. She was *exactly* that kind of woman. She was

sensuous, even when sipping the wine she'd been handed, with a voluptuous figure. Miss Wright was exceptionally attractive and probably fought off hordes of men at every turn, but he would not be one of them. He could admire her beauty, but he didn't *want* her. Not anything like he wanted Olivia, who'd just glanced his in direction and was now walking toward him.

"Josephine? Darien?" Olivia said. "I'd like to introduce you to an old friend of the Gentry family and a childhood friend of Matt's, Jim Somerset."

Both Wrights turned, and Darien barked a laugh.

"Dear Lord! I thought Adam's baby brother was huge, but he's near petite beside Mr. Somerset." Darien stretched out his hand. "Pleased to meet you. This is my sister, Josephine."

Jim nodded to the sister and turned to shake Darien's hand. "I was bigger and smarter than him even when we were boys."

"Ha!" Darien said with a laugh. "And a dry sense of humor, too!"

THE DOOR TO THE MAIN ROOM FLEW OPEN AND ADAM CAME IN, bringing the cold air with him. Olivia could hear Jenny in the hallway telling someone to shut the door and get Mr. Adam's cases to his room. He was shrugging off his coat, spotted with snowflakes, with Jenny's help.

"Darien!" he said and hurried forward. "It's so good to see you."

The men embraced and slapped each other's backs in greeting.

"Who knew you and I would end up being rather diminutive beside your brother and his friend. That would have never served us well when we were getting into some trouble back in our school days, would it?"

Adam laughed, his eyes twinkling. "You haven't changed a bit."

"I want you to meet my sister," Darien said and turned to take Josephine's hand.

Olivia was watching the reunion and saw when Adam turned to look at Josephine Wright His smile slowly faded. He opened his mouth but said nothing.

Josephine held out her perfectly manicured hand. "Darien has talked of you so often over the years, I feel as if I already know you. I am so happy to finally make your acquaintance in person."

Adam swallowed, looked at her hand, and stood mute. His hand came from his side, ever so slowly, palm up, to hold hers lightly. He kissed the back of her hand and straightened, staring all the while at her. Josephine's cheeks turned pink and she blinked slowly.

"How gallant," she said in a breathy voice.

"Well," Eleanor Gentry broke in. "Let me get you a glass of wine, Adam. How was your trip?"

Adam looked at his mother as if he'd just noticed her. "Mother," he said and kissed her cheek. "Is there whiskey?"

Matt poured a drink from a crystal decanter and handed it to his brother. He leaned forward and whispered as he did. Olivia couldn't hear what he said but imagined he was telling Adam to compose himself, although Adam continued to dart glances at his friend's sister. He swallowed the whiskey handed him in one swift gulp.

"Tell me about Paradise," Darien said. "It's every bit as beautiful as you described it all those years ago."

"I'll give you the grand tour tomorrow morning and take you to see the stables, if you'd like," Adam said. "We've added a ballroom and additional bedrooms above it. In fact, I think you are in one of the new ones."

"He's in the blue room, Adam," Eleanor said.

"I'm looking forward to it, and I'm sure Josephine would like to join us," Darien said.

Adam faced her. "I'm hoping so."

"I would love to see more of Paradise and hear its history," she replied.

"Then Aunt Brigid and Mother should take you on a private tour as they are the most familiar," Matt said with a grin, eliciting a growl from Adam, as Matt had surely intended.

Olivia saw Jenny come into the room and speak to her mother. Eleanor walked to Darien and smiled up at him.

"Supper is about to be served. May I have your escort?"

"Certainly!" he said and winged his arm for her to take.

Matt escorted Annie while he pushed Aunt Brigid's wheeled chair.

"Olivia?" Jim said.

She looked up at him and smiled, glad that he was here with her family, and happy to wrap her arm around his. They walked past Adam and Josephine Wright, who were still staring at each other.

"Adam?" she said over her shoulder. "Are you coming?"

"Yes," he said and took the hand Josephine held out and placed it on his arm and turned to the door. "Miss Wright?"

"I thought this visit with the Gentrys was meant to be informal. I've already given leave to your family to call me Josephine."

"I think it's best for me to be less informal where you're concerned, ma'am," Adam said as he followed them to the dining room.

JIM ENJOYED THE EVENING WITH THE GENTRYS EVEN MORE than he'd anticipated. He was able to gaze at Olivia without causing any alarm simply because she was across the table from him. He'd seen Mrs. Gentry watching him several times, although she did nothing but raise one eyebrow in his direction. Was it a signal? Should he leave off looking at her daughter? He couldn't even if he tried, which he had no intention of doing. There was some elemental pull at work between his eyes and Olivia's face.

Darien Wright was entertaining her and the others now and had several times over dinner. He was charming and handsome and told humorous stories about Adam and himself that had everyone at the table laughing.

"Won't you accompany us on the tour of your lovely home and stables tomorrow, Olivia?" Darien said.

"Yes, certainly!" she said.

He watched her smile and laugh and then turn her head to face him. What he would give to have her light up like the flicker of a hundred candles when she looked at him, but instead her smile slowly faded and a blush climbed her cheeks. He picked up his fork and took a bite of the bourbon cake that had just been placed in front of him.

"Josephine," Eleanor said. "I've read about your salons in Washington. Is it true that you have had senators and governors as your guests?"

"It is. Politicians attend, as well as literary figures and other interesting people," she said. "You should visit me, Eleanor. I would love to host you and your daughter and daughter-in-law."

"I don't know about Annie traveling that far," Matt said quickly.

"It was just an invitation, Matt," Olivia said. "Annie may or may not want to attend. I would, though."

Annie looked at her husband. "I'm not an invalid."

"Yes, but . . ." he said and looked down at his plate.

"I'd be delighted to have you. Are you interested in women's suffrage?" Josephine asked Olivia.

"Yes, I am. I do not understand why women aren't allowed to vote. It's ludicrous!" she replied.

"I agree." Josephine leaned forward in her seat to see Olivia's face. "Please say you'll come."

"You haven't asked any of the men at the table to attend," Adam said and sipped his wine.

Josephine looked at him from where she sat on his left. "My houseguests are always of the female persuasion. The reputation of my salons must be above reproach and therefore so must I."

"No hotels in Washington?" Adam asked and glanced at her.

Matt looked up from his plate to his brother. "Why would you want to travel all those miles to sit and listen to the chatter at a *salon*?"

"Sometimes you don't have the brains God gave you, Matthew," Aunt Brigid said.

"Maybe I'm interested in a sophisticated conversation now and again," Adam said and grinned. "And maybe I could visit with my old friend Darien at the same time."

"I'd be delighted to have you join me at my bachelor lodgings just a few miles from Josephine's home," Darien said and looked at Olivia. "I'd be happy to escort the ladies to some of the more famous sites around Washington as well."

Olivia smiled and clasped her hands under her chin. "That would be wonderful, wouldn't it, Mother? Oh, Annie, you must come along. I would like to hear what our representatives have to say and try and change their minds when I disagree!"

"About what?" Annie asked.

"About everything. About suffrage and the treatment of soldiers after the war. Things I've read about. Things that will matter to all of us," she said, leaning forward in her seat.

It was at that moment, as Jim looked at her, at her sparkling eyes and shining lips and rosy cheeks, that he realized he was reaching too far above himself. He was not material for a capital visit—he was a farrier. He'd always be a farrier. He had no intention of moving away from his family or from his hometown. His dreams were smaller than hers. A home, a peaceful future, a wife, children, and a continuation of everything that was comfortable about his life. She was meant for something bigger, something grander—that was clear.

All his chest beating and sadness of earlier months had been replaced by hope and want, yet he knew now that his dreams were misplaced. That her hopes and wants were beyond his reach, his ability, and even his temperament. He could no sooner relegate her to an uneventful existence without meaning beyond her sphere than throw her from a cliff.

Mrs. Gentry rose from her seat, and the gentlemen followed. "I believe we can enjoy some cordials in the main room and have a song or two if Aunt Brigid will play for us."

He waited until everyone else had exited the dining room and then asked Jenny for his coat. He was pulling it on in the hallway when Olivia came through the doors from the main room.

"Oh. Are you leaving?" she asked.

"I am." He pulled a scarf around his neck. He didn't want to look at her but he finally had to, to thank her.

"It's been a lovely evening. Please give your mother and your company my regrets." She was looking at him with worry and maybe disappointment. "I've a busy day tomorrow and want to start early."

"Will you be at church on Sunday?"

He shook his head slowly, looking at her, memorizing her face, knowing he must give her up even if he'd never really had her. "I will not," he said and put his hat on his head and turned to the door. He turned back to her, his throat raw, his stomach rumbling. He picked up her hand and rubbed his thumb over the back of it, feeling the heat and softness of her skin, smelling the rose scent that surrounded her. He looked into her eyes. "Enjoy your stay in Washington. I'm sure you'll be able to change any minds you set yours to. You're exceedingly bright and well . . . just as beautiful. Good night."

It felt like good-bye. It was.

CHAPTER 10

"Why did Jim leave early last night? Did you see him before he left?" Adam asked her the following morning in the dining room.

The Wrights had not come downstairs yet, and Adam and she were sipping coffee. "He said he needed to be up early today."

"Strange that he didn't come into the main room. He seemed to be enjoying himself."

"I thought so, too." She leaned against the window frame, looking outside but seeing nothing. "I thought he wanted to be here," she whispered.

Adam leaned against the other side of the window. "Maybe he did. Maybe he just had to get up early."

She shook her head. "I don't think so."

Something had happened. Something had changed, and she didn't know what it was or why he wouldn't say anything to her. She'd lain awake that night thinking of what she'd said and what others had said. He'd called her bright and beautiful. He'd said it reverently. She could hear his voice in his head, a soft but deep intonation that rumbled through her head and carried on to her chest, lingering there and wrapping itself around her heart.

She spent much of the day entertaining the Wrights with her

mother and Adam. She found herself alone a few times with Darien. He was interesting and humorous and extremely clever. She laughed more than she had in a long time, and it felt good to be lighthearted, and even silly, forcing her mind away from her troubles, if only for a short time.

"When do you think you'll be visiting my sister?" he asked and grinned as she escorted him on a tour of Paradise. "I admit, I'm impatient to show you the capital and make every man in the city jealous of me while you are on my arm."

She shook her head and smiled. "You are ridiculous with your outrageous compliments, even if I enjoy receiving them! But I'm thinking of the spring. It makes traveling so much easier when the weather is fine."

"The Washington and Atlantic Railroad stops in Winchester and will bring you directly in to the city. I'll meet you and your mother and sister-in-law at the train station and take you to Josephine's. December is generally temperate."

"I'll have to speak to my mother about the trip and when it would be most convenient for her to be away."

Darien stepped a little closer. He smiled ruefully. "Would I earn a slap if I said I will count the days until you arrive?"

"I doubt a busy man like yourself will be concerned with a friend's sibling more than a few moments after he is once again among the sophisticated ladies in our capital."

He sobered. He looked at her hands clasped at her waist and touched them with his until she laid them in his palms. "Although it pains me to disagree with a lady, you are wrong," he said and looked her in the eyes. He tilted his head as he looked at her closely. "Unless of course, there is someone special in your life already."

Olivia looked away. "I . . . I . . . there is no one."

"Not even Mr. Somerset?"

"No," she said and felt a blush rise on her cheeks. "Not Mr. Somerset."

"Ah, I've steered away from our lighthearted conversations and made you frown. Would you show me the Paradise library?"

Wright winged his arm and proceeded to tell her a funny story about Adam having become lost in his college's library. Eleanor joined them and invited him to have coffee and cakes with her in the main room.

Olivia excused herself and went up the staircase. She became aware of muted voices ahead of her around the corner and down the hallway that led to Adam's rooms. At first, she thought it was two of the servants, but then she realized it was a man talking to a woman and it would be very unlikely that a male employee was on the second floor of the house. Olivia looked up and saw a reflection in the large mirror over the table against the wall of the hallway. She could see it was Josephine and Adam standing just in front of the door to his rooms. They were talking softly, and Josephine laughed at something Adam had said. Why did Olivia believe it had been wicked?

She knew she should turn away, but she was caught, mesmerized as she watched her older brother and this exceptionally attractive woman speak to each other in low tones. They stood bare inches apart, and she watched Adam as he inched his face closer and closer to Josephine's. She brought her hand to his face, stroked his cheek, and ran a thumb across his lip. She smiled then and turned away from him, and began walking toward Olivia. Adam called out to her, and she laughed in response but didn't stop walking.

"I will confirm that later," Adam said.

Josephine smiled and continued walking. Olivia turned and hurried into her rooms. She leaned back on the closed door and thought about what she'd seen. There was an intensity between her brother and Josephine Wright, something private and intimate, and maybe wanton, that she shouldn't have been privy to but she couldn't have turned away from for any amount of money or even a Morgan stallion. It was exactly the way she felt when she looked at Jim Somerset and nothing like she felt when she looked at any other man. She'd been devastated when he left right after dinner on Saturday night just when she thought there might be hope for the two of them. She'd been wrong. Again.

* * *

"WOULD YOU . . . WOULD YOU LIKE TO HAVE SUPPER WITH ME this evening?" Jim asked Marabelle Winston as he stood at the counter in her father's store, late November. She looked up at him in confusion.

"Why?" she asked finally.

He couldn't help but wonder why a woman he was asking to spend time with, maybe court if supper invitations led that far, wasn't smiling, not the least bit happy from what he could tell. She'd kissed him at the party last summer at Paradise, hadn't she?

"What do you mean, 'why'?"

She shook her head. "No, but thank you for asking." She turned away to busy herself at the shelves behind her.

"Is there a reason? Something you can tell me?"

Marabelle looked over her shoulder at him and straightened slowly. She looked angry now. Very angry. She looked around the store and motioned him to the far end of the counter. He followed and watched as she stared out the window of the store, opened her mouth to speak, and stopped.

"I've spent my life half in love with you, or even all the way in love with you. I don't remember a time I didn't love you. But I'm determined to forget you. I won't be second fiddle to another woman," she whispered finally.

He felt the color drain from his face. "I don't know who you mean."

"It's getting easier to stop loving you by the minute, Jim," she said with sarcasm. "Of course, you know who I mean. Olivia

Gentry. I don't want a husband who's thinking of another woman while we eat dinner together or go to church or . . . get in bed."

"I'm sorry to have bothered you, Marabelle."

She stared at him for a few long seconds and then turned and walked away, calling out to a customer to see if they needed help. He opened the door to the whipping wind and blowing snow. He made his way across the street and down two blocks. He shoveled the walkway up to his family home and to the business, too, although the forge's heat kept it mostly clear, all the while thinking about his conversation with Marabelle. He looked up at the gray sky and thought this snow might just go on forever and a day from the looks of it. He had Phillip clean the coal chute off and carry extra wood into the house to the rooms that still had working fireplaces. His mother and sisters were in the kitchen with Helen cooking and baking.

Jim stood leaning on the shovel handle, letting the snow build up on his shoulders and head, thinking about taking Marabelle to a marriage bed. Would he blow out all the lamps and candles so that he could imagine it was Olivia's face he kissed, breast he touched, and body he entered? He wasn't certain Marabelle was wrong, and that would be a sad and unhappy start to a lifetime of marriage.

* * *

"WHAT DO YOU THINK, ADAM?" ELEANOR ASKED AS BEATRICE cleared their dinner plates. "Would the first week of January suit you? We could go on Wednesday, be present for Miss Wright's salon on Friday, and leave on the Monday following. We would have time to see the sights and perhaps do some shopping."

"That suits me fine, although I'll have to be home by Tuesday at the latest. I promised Matt I would travel with him to Bridgewater to finalize the sale of Annie's property that is scheduled for that week."

"Can't you use a lawyer for that and avoid the trip?"

"I would like to Mother, but I've advised Matt that one of us should be there. Annie knows no one in Bridgewater she trusts who would be a help in something like this, and I hardly blame her. Matt's arranged a document to stand as her legal representative for the purchase, and he's concerned there may be some language shenanigans that he won't understand. I told him I'd go. We'll be there and back in three days if all goes well and the train schedule is true to what we've been told."

"That will be quite a bit of traveling in a short time," Eleanor said. "Olivia and I will be fine on our own taking the train to Washington."

Adam smiled. "Not to worry. I'll bear up just fine and look forward to seeing Darien again. I'd like to stay closer in touch with him since we've seen each other after nine years apart."

"Is there anyone else you wished to see?" Eleanor smiled.

Adam grinned. "I wouldn't know to whom you are referring."

"Do those dates suit you, Olivia?" Eleanor asked.

"Yes. I've nothing planned." *Ever*, she thought.

"You were quite looking forward to it earlier, dear. If you don't want to go, we don't have to," Eleanor said as she looked at her daughter's face.

Olivia shook her head. "I am looking forward to it. I've received a letter from Josephine detailing all the interesting things we may see and do there. Perhaps I'll want to live there."

Eleanor laid down her fork. "Live there?"

"A young woman cannot live on her own in a large city such as Washington," Adam said.

"Why not?" she asked. "Perhaps I will find a circle of friends there. I may be introduced to people or endeavors that we wish to invest in."

Adam shook his head. "Certainly, you understand that would be impossible."

"And why is that impossible?" she asked as she poured cream in her coffee.

"Because unmarried women do not live alone in a large city, that is why."

"Really?" she said.

"Really! It's not safe, and surely you understand young women must guard their reputations. There are unsavory characters who would assume a woman alone must be open to . . . liaisons," he said.

Olivia had rarely seen her brother in such a state. He was a smart and polished negotiator who found it unnecessary to be emotional, always sticking to facts and figures and delivering them in a way that made others feel as if a subject had been their idea. Eleanor's brows shot up as her sense of proper behavior, especially at the dinner table, was being tested.

"Liaisons?" she repeated.

"My apologies, Mother," he said. "But certainly, you agree."

"Josephine Wright lives alone, Adam. Do you imagine her reputation is in tatters for it, as men consider her open to liaisons?" Olivia asked.

Adam picked up his coffee cup and sipped. "That is hardly comparable."

"But why? Why are her circumstances any different than mine?"

"Because you are my sister and she is not," Adam said. "We will go to Washington. We will *all* come back from Washington."

Olivia was not going to argue any longer. If she decided that a change of location would be the thing to bring her out of the megrims then she would speak to her mother about it. She wasn't a child, contrary to what Adam thought, and he wasn't her parent. She had saved every dividend she'd received from the Paradise business and had quite a nest egg built up. She imagined she could purchase or rent a town house, even in a fashionable section of town, and still be comfortable and able to retain a few employees.

She was desperate, she'd realized of late, to get away from Winchester and all the shadows cast by unworthy men. To leave everything she loved as well, including Paradise and the horses and her family. And a man that would never be hers.

"Saturday next, Adam," she heard her mother say as she realized she'd drifted off into her own mind as she'd done often of late.

"What is Saturday next, Mother?" she asked.

"The Christmas party at the Somersets'. I thought I mentioned it to you."

"You did mention it. Are we going?"

"I've already replied that we'd be there."

Olivia blew out a breath. How she hated seeing Jim. Hated it. He reminded her of all of her errors, especially the fresh one when they'd had a meal together and he'd come to Paradise for dinner. She'd let hope grow between those two occasions and been excited and joyful and anticipating every next moment and hour. When he'd looked at her the way he had when he'd walked in the door that evening as if she were the center of his world, she'd thought their futures would begin to be entwined, that her dreams of being loved by him were within her reach. But something over the course of dinner had changed his mind.

She'd been discouraged and embarrassed when it was apparent that Mr. Dunderage had his sights set on her inheritance. Her confidence had been shaken when it was clear that Mr. Armsworth wanted to use her for the influence her family had and as an ornament for his arm. But this . . . this change in Jim Somerset, this reversal from their meal together in town to coffee at the end of dinner at Paradise had changed her, too. She was no longer so much concerned with what other people thought of her. She was concerned with what she thought of herself. And there must be something terribly wrong with her to elicit that change in him.

* * *

"Everything is delicious, Mrs. Somerset, and decorated so beautifully," Olivia said as she met with her hostess near the buffet that had been laid out in the dining room of the Somerset home. There was pine draped everywhere, rum punch with cinnamon filling the air with a wonderful aroma, and red bows at every corner in every room of the house.

"I am so glad you're enjoying it, dear. I haven't seen you in town or at church lately."

Olivia smiled. "I've just been so busy lately it seems."

"Seeing much of Mr. Armsworth?"

"No. I haven't spoken to Mr. Armsworth since the harvest dance," she said and looked at her hands.

"Well, all the girls are wondering if you and he are no longer . . . interested in each other. I imagine there are one or two young ladies in town who would like to set their sights on him but would not want things to be awkward."

"They are welcome to him, Mrs. Somerset. But I would caution them that Mr. Armsworth is not exactly what he appears to be."

"Oh. Dear me. I'm so sorry if I've upset you," she said and looked at Olivia inquisitively.

"You've not, ma'am"—Olivia attempted to smile—"I am quite happy to be parted from him permanently."

Mrs. Somerset laid a hand on her arm and looked at her with a gentle concern. "You're looking pale, Olivia, and a little thinner since I saw you last. If there's something troubling you, you should talk to your mother or your sister-in-law. That is the same advice that I give all my children. It does us no good, no good at all, to keep feelings and worries inside."

Olivia shook her head and felt tears spring to her eyes. What was the matter with her? This was Mrs. Somerset! She'd known the woman all of her life and knew she was kind and a good and loving mother to her children. She nearly blurted it out, here in the middle of a lovely holiday party. She would cry on the woman's shoulder and tell her that her son was causing her pain and distress and that she was going to move away from everything she knew just to put an end to it—if she wasn't careful of her feelings and her tongue.

"Here you are, Olivia," Annie said at that moment. "The music is going to start, won't you come into the other room?"

"Oh, yes! Jane has been practicing all week! She is very nervous but excited to be playing for all of our guests," Mrs. Somerset said.

"I'm sure she'll be just dandy," Annie said and smiled and looked around the room. "You have a very nice house. So homey. It's my first time here."

Mrs. Somerset chuckled. "Your husband was here as much as he was home when he was a boy and as a young man, too. He and Jim were constant companions, and Olivia was here often, too, seeing Nettie and Emmaline."

"It's so wonderful that your families are so close. I didn't have friends like this growing up," Annie said. "But I think our little one will have plenty of friends here in Winchester."

Mrs. Somerset put her hand on Annie's cheek. "Well, I don't know why I've never thought of it before but you must become acquainted with my oldest daughter, Nettie, and her husband John. Matthew knows them both well, of course. They have two children, Rachel and Albert, precious grandchildren for me. How wonderful if our families stayed close!"

"It would be wonderful. Don't you think so, Livie?" Annie asked.

"Um, yes, yes of course," she said. She desperately wanted to be gone from this conversation, from the room, and even the house. She didn't want to talk about families and closeness and babies. Especially not here where corners and doorways held memories.

"Mother," Jim said as he approached. "I think Jane is wanting Betsy to turn her pages for her, and Betsy is busy speaking to her friends."

"Oh, dear. Jane will be in a panic. Excuse me, girls."

"Annie. Olivia," he said with a nod. "I hope you're enjoying yourselves."

"Matt is waving to me from the other room," Annie said and turned away in a hurry.

All the guests had left the dining room as the music began in the parlor. She was left to stare at him, and her eyes burned with tears she would not allow to fall. "I'm going to Washington to visit Josephine Wright the first week of January."

He nodded and licked his lips. "I'm sure you'll enjoy yourself."

"I'm sure I will."

He was staring back at her, and now she was looking everywhere but his face. The lump in her throat and the tears in her eyes were quickly turning to anger and frustration. "Why did you leave early that night?"

"I told you. I had to be up early."

"I don't believe you."

He shrugged. "I'm sorry to hear that."

She was going to disgrace herself soon, either throwing herself in his arms or bursting into tears or slapping his face, she wasn't sure which. But anger was creeping up her spine, anger and humiliation, that she continued to want this man who clearly did not want her.

"My plans are to move to Washington. Permanently."

He looked away, and when he looked back his eyes were glittering. "What a fool thing to do."

"I've always been a fool," she whispered.

He stepped closer to her, looming over her, forcing her to tilt her head back to look at him. The rage in his eyes was gone, replaced with something else. Something softer or regretful. "I'm not . . . I'm not part of that world. I'll never be. I'm a farrier."

She shook her head. "What are talking about?"

"The night I left early from dinner at Paradise. I'm not like the Wrights or like Adam or you. I don't intend to try and influence anyone, let alone the men who guide this country. I work for a living and I like it."

"What does that have to do with anything? No one was asking you to."

"You're meant for great things, Olivia. I'm meant for Winchester."

"So, you have to be one or the other? You can't be a farrier and be involved in the politics of our country? You can't enjoy a dinner conversation about important issues and know how to shape a horse's shoe? How ridiculous you are!"

She turned to leave, but he grabbed her arm and turned her to him. He opened his mouth to speak and then wrinkled his nose and forehead. He was parsing out a dilemma, it was clear. She wouldn't be around when he determined his answer. She broke his hold on her and followed the laughter and music until she found her mother chatting with Annie.

JIM WAS FUMING. HE WASN'T LISTENING TO HIS SISTER'S PIANO playing or seeing the dancers just ahead of him. He was unable to think of anything other than what Olivia had just said to him. His hope that he'd be left alone until he was able to calm himself would not be fulfilled. Adam slung an arm around his shoulders. It was all he could do to keep from punching him in the nose.

"How's my sister?" Adam said.

Jim jerked his head to him. "Going to move to Washington, I hear."

"I don't like it any more than you do."

"It's in your power to do something about it. She can't live there alone."

"That's exactly how I feel, but Olivia isn't just any woman.

She's very special, very bright. My mother asked me if there was a reason why I didn't think Olivia could be successful at anything she chose to do. Mother is right, of course. Not everyone has as much reason to stay in Winchester as you and I do, though," Adam said. "Olivia needs to find her place in the world, as mother says, and she's decided to find it in Washington."

"It will be dangerous for a woman in a big city."

"It will be. But I've got to trust her and her good sense and upbringing."

"That's not good enough."

Adam looked at him wryly and slapped him on the back. "You could always marry her. You'd at least have a say then. Not that she'd listen to you all that much."

He opened and closed his mouth several times but no words were forthcoming. What Adam had said was the dream he fell asleep to and his greatest hope, even if he had relegated it to some dark, unseen corner of his mind.

"I'm sure she'll meet lots of important people while she's there. Maybe she'll marry one of *them*," Jim said, with barely concealed anger.

Adam stared at him until he looked at him. "I didn't realize how bad you had it."

"I don't know what you're talking about," he replied and walked away. He could still hear Adam's laughter in the next room.

CHAPTER 11

Adam, Eleanor, and Olivia stepped off the Washington and Atlantic train in the late afternoon on an unseasonably warm Wednesday in January. Darien Wright was waiting and greeted them while their baggage was brought to the station.

"My man will take care of your luggage, Eleanor. Don't worry. My carriage is here to take us to Josephine's. We will have you settled in no time," he said. "How was the train ride?"

"Fine, but we did have to stop twice for problems with the track. It was scheduled to be a three-hour trip, but as you know it took us every bit of four to get here," Adam said.

"We were comfortable the whole time," Eleanor said. "It was all modern, and the conductor was very gracious."

"Of course, we were in a semiprivate car, Mother," Olivia said and smiled at Darien.

He laughed. "Of course, you were! My friend Adam would not like traveling with the throngs! He would insist on traveling in style."

"Come on, Wright," Adam said, laughing and grabbed him by the back of the neck. "Lead on and show us your carriage."

"May I say that both of you ladies look lovely," Darien said once they were seated.

Eleanor smiled. "Thank you, sir."

He was looking at Olivia appreciatively, and she smiled at him. "Even after four hours of traveling? You are too kind!"

"All true! Josephine is very excited to have you visit her. She doesn't often have houseguests." He looked at Adam. "And you and I will rattle around in my bachelor town house, drinking whiskey later into the night than advisable and discussing all matters that are for men's ears only."

Adam chuckled. "I nod off in front of my fireplace before ten in the evening these days. We aren't young college men any longer!"

"For four days, we will pretend it isn't so. We will sleep late in the morning and carouse until midnight," Darien said and looked at Eleanor. "You are no doubt worried that I will be a poor influence on your son."

"My son is a man in his own right and will not be influenced beyond his comfort, but I imagine it may be a challenge with the enticements of lazy mornings and late nights when there may be unsavory characters about," she said with a smile.

Darien shot a look at Adam with slumped shoulders and barely a grin. "Your mother does know how to take the wind from the sails of a man yearning for his youth."

"She does," Adam said.

"Here we are," Darien said as the carriage drew to halt.

The front door of the house opened and Josephine hurried out. "I've been waiting for you to arrive," she said with a smile as she took Eleanor's hand and reached for Olivia's. "Please come in. I am so excited to see you!"

Darien bussed his sister's cheek and carried luggage inside. Olivia looked up and saw Adam staring at Josephine, seemingly oblivious to whatever else was happening around him.

"Miss Wright," he said and tipped his hat.

A blush climbed up Josephine's neck to her cheeks. "Mr. Gentry."

Darien came back out of the house and slapped Adam on the back. "Come on. We're to my apartments for a nap and a nip. We're dining here tonight, and Josephine's cook is exceptional."

"'Til this evening, ladies," Adam said and followed his friend into the carriage. Josephine watched him go.

Olivia could see the entranceway's marble floors and high ceilings led to several rooms on the first floor, the hallways all painted in light colors with gray and rose accents and dark furniture. Josephine led them up the staircase, followed by the housekeeper and two young men carrying their luggage.

When everyone was gone from her room, Olivia washed her face and hands and sat down at the writing desk between two tall, narrow windows overlooking a small courtyard. She could see the backs of other homes through the bare branches of the trees. If she decided to move to Washington, she would have to accustom herself to being in such close proximity to other homes and people. It would be very different for her, she realized.

But it would be wonderful to plan her own household decorating. Paradise was all earthy tones and solid waxed woods. She loved it there, it was home and warm and safe, but it would be exciting to staff a house and choose the colors and the furnishings. She plopped her chin in her hand. She'd always thought she'd plan a home with a husband, that she'd have a partner to consult, but she wasn't sure of that any longer, nor was she sure of herself, sadly.

Darien Wright was an interesting and attractive man, but her insides didn't roll over when he was around and she had no intention of encouraging a relationship with him other than friendship. He would be a good friend to her, especially if she chose to move nearby, but she didn't want any romantic entanglements with anyone until she began to feel herself again. She couldn't predict when that might be. She was just not feeling herself and little had interested her in the last few weeks. She was hoping the change of scenery and setting would pique her interest.

She kicked off her shoes and curled up in a large, soft chair. She closed her eyes and didn't open them until a maid came in her room announcing the party would be gathering in the parlor soon.

"THERE SHE IS!" DARIEN SAID AS OLIVIA CAME THROUGH THE open double doors into a large well-lit room with several seating areas and papered walls with an ivy design.

She accepted a glass of sherry and smiled. "I admit, I napped in the most comfortable chair I've ever sat in."

"Traveling can be so tiresome," Josephine said and turned to include Eleanor. "I wanted to let you know what I've planned for us for the next few days. Of course, my salon is on Friday evening, but we've got tomorrow and Saturday and Sunday. I'd like to take you to the dining rooms at the Occidental Hotel in Washington on Saturday. What would you ladies like to do?"

"I'd like to do some shopping for my son Matthew's new home. I've promised his wife Annie that I will look at some furniture and china and perhaps bring back samples or pictures for her to choose," Eleanor said.

"Shopping will be no hardship for me," Josephine said with a laugh. "Although, it won't be complete unless we visit some dress shops I know. Is there something special you'd like to do, Olivia?"

She glanced at Eleanor and Adam. "Yes, there is. Do you know where the Clover Hill School for Young Ladies is located? I do have the directions written down upstairs in my bag."

Darien turned from Adam. "I know where it is. Not far, actually. Maybe a mile or so as you go out of town."

"That will be no problem. We could go Saturday morning if that suits. May I ask why you are interested in Clover Hill?" Josephine gave her a quizzical look.

"I've been reading newspapers out of Washington when they

are available and looking at the prices of houses and row homes. Clover Hill has run an advertisement for someone to teach riding to their pupils a few days a week. I thought I might investigate while I am here," she said.

Adam was looking into the glass he held and clinking the chips of ice against the crystal. Her mother was looking at her in her normal serene manner. Darien Wright was smiling broadly.

"Are you thinking of moving here, then?" he asked.

"Yes. Yes, I am," she said.

"You are interested in teaching equitation?" Josephine asked.

"I am. I like to be active, and if I decided to live on my own, I don't see myself being satisfied with visiting and shopping. I'll need something to do, I think."

"You really are seriously considering this?" Darien asked.

"Yes."

He smiled at her. "I haven't had such good news in forever."

"This is quite a surprise," Josephine said. "I didn't know you were thinking about moving here, although I am thrilled. What brought on this interest in Washington?"

She didn't know what to say. She had no interest in Washington particularly other than it was not Winchester and Jim Somerset wasn't in it. "I've been thinking of moving to a city for some time. Your visit and stories of Washington prompted me to begin investigating what I could expect here, if and when I decided to move."

"What do you think of Olivia's plans, Eleanor?" Josephine asked.

"I will miss her terribly if she does decide to move, and I'm not sure I like the idea of her being in the city alone, but Olivia is bright and self-sufficient, and her own person. She'll make up her own mind."

"I think it's a terrible idea, even though no one has asked me," Adam said. "But Mother is right. Olivia must make up her own mind about the direction of her life, even if it is dangerous."

"Come now," Darien said with a chuckle. "You must recognize that Olivia is an adult and this is 1872. Are we not modern enough yet that a woman can be safe and happy if she is careful and has her wits about her? This is not the Wild West, and she would have friends here."

"I am just starting to think seriously about this change for myself. The Clover Hill position appeared in the last paper I was able to read before coming here, and I thought perhaps it was a lucky coincidence or maybe providence."

"There is no luck about it," Adam muttered.

"Not very supportive of you," Darien said. "It's not as if she's moving across an ocean. She would be able to visit often, and you could visit her as much."

"It's a very exciting city, and you are just the type of woman that would take it by storm. I would be thrilled to call you friend and have you nearby," Josephine said. "We would have such fun!"

"It's the everyday living that I would miss," Eleanor said and patted Olivia's hand. "But time marches on, and Olivia is a young woman of a new generation who is intent on making a mark. I'm jealous of her and terrified for her all at the same time."

She glanced at her mother and looked away quickly. Tears sprang to her eyes. Her mother jealous? The woman she worshipped and stood in awe of? The woman who survived a kidnapping, married a stranger, raised a family, nursed the love of her life until his death, all while instilling a heightened sense of honor and insisting on ladylike behavior was jealous of her? How could she continue this farce? She couldn't. She couldn't let them think she was some perfect individual when she was in fact a coward.

She stood and walked to the marble fireplace, her hands trembling. "I'm not what you think, nor are my motives noble. I'm not moving toward what I think is high-minded and exciting society. I wish to move away, run actually, from unhappiness, from a situation . . . that will always be in Winchester. It will stay and I will go."

The room was silent other than the deep breaths she herself was taking. She felt an arm slide around her as Adam kissed her forehead.

"I am a firm believer that things do work out for the best in the end and this will, too," he said quietly but then continued to the others in the room, "I am also so hungry, I could eat everything on that sideboard of nibbles but would prefer to sit down to a many course meal. Have I embarrassed you and Mother with my poor manners?"

She laughed softly and touched the corner of her eyes. "You haven't embarrassed me."

"A hungry man!" Josephine said as she stood. "We must feed him immediately before he begins eating the drapes!"

* * *

"I could write an ode to your beauty, Miss Gentry," the bespectacled fellow said to her as they stood chatting in the parlor.

"Please, do not, Mr. Finchlot," Olivia said with a smile. "Ladies do not like to draw attention to themselves, as I'm sure you know."

"The reader would never know who the poem was about. I would change your name, and it would be our secret."

"Changing my name would be helpful, I think, as little rhymes with Olivia."

Mr. Finchlot looked momentarily perplexed. "You are right. This will be a challenge, but it will be worth it for you to know how your beauty and kindness have affected me."

She didn't smile. "Thank you, Mr. Finchlot. I believe my mother needs me."

She wound her way among Josephine's guests to the dining room laid out lavishly with thinly sliced beef and cheeses and platters of sweets. It was a lovely party, she thought, even knowing few guests, but all in all it reminded her very much of socials in Winchester. Adam was standing with three men talking quietly and seriously and she saw her mother speaking to several men and a few women.

"Here is my daughter, Olivia," Eleanor said, smiling and reaching out her hand. "I was just saying your father and I were blessed with three extraordinary children."

Introductions were made, and Olivia noticed several of the older men vying for her mother's attention. Eleanor was animated and charming and it was wonderful to see such a fuss made of her and to see her smile in such a carefree, cheerful way.

"We were discussing the poor veterans from the war, Olivia, and I know you have some firm opinions on the matter," she said.

"I'd like to hear them, Miss Gentry," Jessup Hendrix said. "I'm always interested in hearing our young citizens' views."

Olivia found herself at the center of a spirited conversation. Not everyone at the gathering was respectful and measured, but Josephine or her brother quickly settled outbursts. She even saw Darien escort one red-faced young man to the door.

When the last guest left and Darien and Adam wished them good night she, Eleanor, and Josephine sat together in the sitting room attached to Josephine's bedroom. Josephine was in a voluminous and frilly pale yellow nightgown and robe, Eleanor had kicked off her shoes, and Olivia had let down her hair. She sat on the floor in front of Eleanor as her mother brushed it.

"What a lovely evening," Eleanor said. "I wasn't sure what to expect, but I can't remember when I've enjoyed myself as much."

Olivia tilted her head back to see her mother's face and smiled. "Mr. Hendrix and Mr. McKellar were enjoying themselves in your company certainly."

Eleanor shook her head. "Hardly, dear. They were very polite, though, and so gentlemanly."

Josephine smiled. "Every man in the room was asking me who you both were. Hendrix and McKellar were very attentive, Eleanor, which is a bit unusual for both of them. Hendrix never married and is seen about town with a variety of ladies his own age, rarely the same one twice. McKellar was widowed a few years ago after a long and happy marriage. He escorts his maiden sister to social events. Both are well-situated financially, respected here, and quite handsome, in my opinion."

Eleanor shrugged but followed with a grin. "I enjoyed their conversation. How was your evening, Olivia?"

"Mr. Finchlot promised to write an ode to me until I pointed out that nothing rhymes with Olivia."

"Oh dear!" Josephine said when she had stopped laughing and wiped her eyes. "That is so typical of poor Edwin Finchlot. He wants very badly to be seen as a romantic hero, but I can rarely notice anything about him other than whatever he has spilled on his shirt."

"It was yellow tonight. I imagine it was the mustard sauce, although I didn't ask him."

They all laughed again, and Olivia thought about how much she'd enjoyed herself so far on their visit. She was very seriously considering setting up a household here as a single woman, and having Josephine as a friend would be lovely.

"Mr. Newton told me as he left that he was very interested in an introduction, Olivia. He was sorry he had to leave early as he was called back to his work at the secretary of state's office. He asked me if we would be 'at home' for visitors on Sunday. I would be very surprised if he didn't arrive on my doorstep at two o'clock sharp in the afternoon."

"Which gentleman was he?" Eleanor asked.

"He is quite tall and brown-haired and so very charming. When he smiles, every debutante within one hundred feet sighs," she said.

"He had on a black waistcoat with pinstripes of silver thread, did he not?" Olivia asked, and Josephine nodded.

"You noticed him then, Olivia?" Eleanor said.

"He is a very handsome man," she replied.

"You sound less than excited about the prospect of meeting him, though," Josephine said.

She shrugged and looked down at her hands. "I'm not interested in any romantic entanglements. Perhaps it's best I stay to my rooms when your guests are visiting."

"Oh," Josephine said softly. "Newton is a gentleman. He would not pursue you if you weren't interested."

Eleanor hugged her from behind and kissed her cheek. "We will shop in the morning and eat a fancy meal at a very popular restaurant in the evening and not worry what the next day will bring."

"You're right, Mother. I'm tired now and will find my bed. Good night, ladies," she said as she stood.

* * *

OLIVIA LAY IN HER BED SUNDAY MORNING WATCHING LARGE fluffy snowflakes tumble past her window and thought about the busy day they'd had yesterday. Shopping for Matt and Annie had put her in mind of her own furniture purchases if she bought a house on her own. She'd seen several beautiful pieces, including a bedroom set that had been painted white. It seemed a waste to cover all that exquisite wood, but the outcome was so gorgeous; that was exactly what she would buy when the time came. Some houses came fully or partially furnished, Josephine had told her, and she supposed she'd have to look at each house and what was included before making a decision, but the dreaming was so nice and kept her mind occupied when it might have wandered into that part of her heart that was crushed. Bruised. Lost.

On the return trip from shopping Darien had the carriage

take them to Clover Hill. It was a magnificent farm and stables, and the headmistress was gracious. The school buildings were well-kept and the young girls there, from eight to seventeen years old, were mannerly and bright, greeting them with youthful exuberance and good manners. There would be a position available come September of the following year, although Miss McNally wished to settle on an applicant by the spring.

Olivia was tempted to ask Darien or Josephine to direct her to an agency that knew of homes for sale even more so than when she'd thought about moving to Washington just to get away from Winchester. It wasn't Winchester she wanted to get away from if she were honest with herself. It was Jim Somerset. The idea of teaching riding to young women appealed to her, too. She'd found solace and challenges and equine friendships as a young girl in the stables of Paradise and would like to pass along her passions and whatever talent she had to offer. She'd talked to the stable master at length, and she could tell he'd been impressed with her knowledge. She'd been able to identify the source of a particularly nasty sore on one of the mares and given them Paradise's salve recipe for treatment. It was a successful interview, from both her perspective and Clover Hill's, she believed.

She was beginning to feel as though a move to Washington might be a path to some happiness and contentment rather than the destination she arrived at as she scurried away from something unpleasant. She turned at a knock at her door and heard her mother's voice from the other side.

"Come in, Mother." She stood, pulling a shawl around her shoulders.

Eleanor was fully dressed, down to her gloves. "Oh, good, you're awake."

"I've been lulling around in this lovely bed watching the snow fall, but you're already dressed and . . . Mother? What is wrong?"

"I received a telegram very early this morning. Aunt Brigid is ill. I've sent for Adam and the two of us are leaving on the nine o'clock train to return to Paradise. I've already spoken to Josephine about you staying here a few more days, and she is very pleased to have your company."

Olivia's breath caught. "Aunt Brigid is sick? How sick, Mother?" she asked and hurriedly pulled her case onto the bed and opened it. "Give me just a few minutes and I will be ready. Why didn't you wake me earlier?"

Eleanor came around the bed and took her hands. "Livie, I've already spoken to Josephine, and she said she will have a maid accompany you on a return trip later this week. You need to be away from things, people, even us, right now, I think. I must get home to Aunt Brigid, but you need to stay here and enjoy the change in routine and company."

"But . . . but what of Aunt Brigid? I can be a help to you while she's sick."

"Yes, you could be a wonderful help, but that is my life, Olivia. You have your own life to live. I think Josephine is good for you, too. She is close to your age, and to look at her you wouldn't think there was much depth to her but that isn't a fair judgment. I believe she would be a good sounding board for you if you chose to share your troubles with her."

Olivia looked away. "I don't have any troubles worth mentioning, Mother. And I would never unburden my insecurities on someone of such a recent acquaintance."

"Perhaps that is the problem, dear. You won't talk to anyone about much of anything." Eleanor leaned forward and kissed both her cheeks. "Stay here and relax. Sort out what needs sorting and then come home with a clear head and maybe a more definite direction. I love you, dear."

"I love you, too, Mother. Please kiss Aunt Brigid for me. Let me dress so I can say good-bye to Adam."

Olivia hurried and then went downstairs. Adam was there, dusting snow from the shoulders of his topcoat and hat, Darien beside him doing the same.

"The snow doesn't seem to be lying much on the roads and walkways," Adam said. "But we should hurry if we are to catch the early train."

"I'll take good care of your sister, Adam," Josephine said.

He walked to her and clasped her outstretched hands. "I'm sure you will. I enjoyed myself very much on this visit. Will you come to Paradise again sometime?"

She smiled. "I would like that. You may write to me, if you wish. Oh, do not look at me that way. As if a man and a woman sharing an occasional letter were somehow as evil as the temptation in the Garden."

"I will not comment on temptations in the presence of my mother and sister," he said, "but will wait impatiently for your first missive."

Darien chuckled, and Eleanor clucked her tongue.

"Adam? We mustn't be late you said," Eleanor said.

"I feel like I should be going with you," Olivia said.

Adam kissed her cheek. "I will get Mother home, and we'll send a telegram straightaway about Aunt Brigid. I'll be leaving Tuesday morning with Matt to settle the selling of Annie's house in Bridgewater, and Annie will be able to help Mother."

"It depends on what is ailing Aunt Brigid, Adam. I think Annie is expecting again, and the doctor will not want her in a sickroom. But I have Jenny, and all the rest of the staff. Please relax and enjoy yourself, Olivia. I don't think her situation is serious, but you know how it is when you are ill. We always want our loved ones close by. Aunt Brigid is the same. She is missing me and I would not let her want for my company. You know she is dear to me and to us all."

"Annie is expecting?" Adam asked.

Olivia nodded, and Eleanor said, "She has not said so but we both think she is."

"I suspect that was why your brother made the comment about her not traveling to Washington on the night of the dinner at Paradise," Josephine said and turned to Olivia. "I'm so very glad you are staying a while longer. We will spend some time lolling about the house, reading and doing nothing more strenuous than walking to the dining room for our meals."

Darien looked at his pocket watch. "We will have to hurry soon."

Olivia hugged her mother and brother and watched them pull away in Darien's carriage. The snow was still falling but it was not terribly cold outside, and she watched as some couples walked and children ran ahead, tongues out, catching flakes.

"Come," Josephine said. "Let us have some breakfast and then we can find comfortable chairs near a fire in the library or the parlor and kick off our shoes."

CHAPTER 12

"Olivia Gentry is moving to Washington?" Emmaline asked her brother as she hurried into the room behind the forge, a bowl of beef stew in her hand. "Here. Eat."

Jim sat down at his desk, picked up the spoon Emmaline had laid beside the bowl, and proceeded to eat. Sometimes he felt as if he were nothing more than a marionette on strings being pulled by the women in his sphere. Someone told him to eat and he ate.

"Where did you hear that about Miss Gentry?" he asked.

"So, we're back to 'Miss Gentry,' are we? Phillip was standing behind you when you and Adam were talking at the Christmas party. Don't blame our little brother. He didn't give that nugget of information up purposefully. I was asking him something else unrelated and he volunteered it, not realizing it was of some note. Phillip will be charming, handsome, spoiled, and a bit of a dupe as an adult."

"You have a cruel streak in you," Jim said.

"What do you know about Olivia moving? I must say I'm terribly jealous. Let alone the fact that she's beautiful, she's apparently a modern freethinker, which is difficult to be in the backwoods of Winchester."

He glanced at his sister.

"What?" she demanded.

"She's selfish, I think. To worry her mother and brothers like this. Mr. Gentry would have never allowed it, that's for sure." He pushed away from his desk. "Thank for bringing me my dinner. I hate tracking all the muck and snow into the house."

"Selfish? By living her life as she sees fit? Even if it isn't to 'Winchester' standards? I'd say she's courageous."

"She's a fool," he said quietly.

"A fool?" Emmaline examined her brother's face even as he tried to turn away from her.

"A selfish fool," he said and looked back at her. "Takes her self off to some city where she knows no one. Where anything could happen to her. Adam and Matt aren't happy about it and Mrs. Gentry isn't, either. For what reason? Does she want an adventure? Does she want more men mooning over her than already do? Does she want her reputation and her family's reputation stained with her childishness?"

"Jim," Emmaline whispered. "That is not why she's going if my guess is right. She's going to start over. You're being judgmental and horrible to her. What is wrong with you?"

"Nothing." He shook his head. "I don't want to talk about her. I'm done with her."

She harrumphed a laugh. "Hardly. You went to dinner at Paradise and have been in a funk ever since. What happened?"

"Nothing happened. I left early because I was meeting someone here the next morning."

"That dinner was a Friday evening. I recall because you were at the house getting Mother to fix your shirt, and she was in the kitchen helping Helen. You were meeting a customer on a Saturday morning?"

"Why don't you go home, Emmaline, and take your questions and your speculations on my private life with you. It's none of your business."

Her mouth closed, stopping her from whatever she was about to say. "I think I will do just that."

* * *

OLIVIA WAS SIPPING WINE, HER FEET PULLED UP UNDER HER, IN front of a crackling fire, Josephine beside her in a like chair and pose.

"I should have a telegram by tomorrow morning at the latest, don't you think?"

"I imagine so. Adam and Eleanor would have arrived home midday. By the time she was able to assess the situation and tell you how your Aunt Brigid was faring, it would have been evening, and I doubt the telegraph office is open Sunday. Where is the closest one?"

"There is one in Winchester. But you're right; Mr. Wither-spoon doesn't open the telegraph office on Sundays."

Olivia was feeling mellowed by thinly sliced filet of beef with red wine sauce that she would have drunk from a glass it was so delicious and chocolate cake with the creamiest chocolate butter-cream icing she'd ever tasted, even better than Mabel's. Thinking of Mabel, though, made her think of Paradise and Paradise made her think of Winchester and Winchester made her think of *him*. What was he doing this evening, she wondered? Had he thought any more of her moving to Washington?

"Why do you suppose it's so difficult for a woman to live her life unmarried?" she said without turning her head.

"Because at our most basic, we need to mate and have children so that we do not become extinct," Josephine said and was quiet a few moments. "It's all we know, too. I mean we, you and I, are the result of a married couple and then our aunts and uncles and friends are married, too."

"I'm fortunate," Olivia replied. "I have enough money and income from our family business that I don't have to worry about food and shelter. There are so few choices for women other than marriage."

"I am fortunate, too. My parents were well situated, and when my father's aunt died their wealth swelled as she left all of her money and properties to them. When my parents passed away, the money came to Darien and me. My portion was held in trust until I was twenty-one and Darien saw to it that I had it outright without his control, which was how it was originally intended."

"Will you ever marry?" Olivia asked. "Pardon. That was far too personal an inquiry."

Josephine looked at her. "We are friends, and if I found a question too personal, I would just choose to not answer it. I'm not sure I'll ever marry. No one has ever stirred my soul. Until recently."

"Adam stirs your soul?"

"I'm not sure yet. Your brother is . . . I find myself focused on him when he is nearby and sometimes when he is far away, too. This is new for me and disconcerting."

"*Focus.* That is an interesting word to use."

"Are you focused on anyone particularly? Mr. Somerset maybe?"

"It's strange. I know many people in Winchester. Ones that work at Paradise. My family. My friends. Acquaintances through church or committees I'm involved with. But I don't think about them, any of them, at random times," Olivia said and turned in her seat to face Josephine. "But I think about him. I'll be doing something completely unrelated to anything and think of him. Of something he's said or a way he's looked at me or of how I feel when he's close by."

"Ah," she said softly. "Is this something new for you?"

She shook her head. "I've been in love with him since I've was twelve years old, I've realized recently. I was courted by some other men, two of whom didn't have honorable intentions, but his face hung in the back of my mind like a shadow even as I declared to myself that I was going to marry another man."

"Have you told him?"

Olivia took a long drink of wine and thought about when she'd kissed him at the creek. She'd been close then to telling him. She shrugged.

"It's hard to be brave, isn't it?" Josephine asked. "There's always the chance that he will look at you and say he would never in a thousand years feel the same. There's a chance we'll be laughed at or worse yet, pitied. And then they would look at us differently forever. Any friendship would then be ruined as it would be an unequal relationship. One who loves and one who does not."

"And as long as I live at Paradise, I will see him with some regularity. There would be no avoiding it."

"Washington began to look very inviting," Josephine said.

"Very much so."

"Wouldn't it be easier to just tell him, though; maybe you wouldn't need to bother moving here. Maybe he would fall at your feet and declare his love," she said and covered a giggle.

Olivia smiled. "I told him once. We are already on that unequal footing."

"Really? When? What happened?"

"I was fifteen. He would have been seventeen or so. I told him I loved him. I told him to wait for me to be old enough to marry him. He was my champion, and he looked at me, stared at me for the longest time, minutes passed, and my excitement and hopefulness in declaring myself to him began to wither. But it didn't occur to me that he didn't feel the same way toward me until he said so. He said he could never marry me. That I was foolish to think it."

Tears welled in her eyes for her young and innocent heart. It seemed impossible to feel such fresh hurt over something that had happened years and years before, but she did. Every time she thought of his voice and words that day her embarrassment and rawness and disappointment and desolation overwhelmed her as it was doing now. Not many weeks after that conversation, she was in the Wilkins' Stable with Timothy Dunderage hoping to forget her declaration to Jim Somerset. She took a deep breath before a gurgle of tears erupted. She finally looked at Josephine.

"You were fifteen? He was seventeen or eighteen? You've been carrying this pain with you since then. have you not?"

Olivia nodded. She didn't trust herself to speak.

Josephine sat her wineglass down on the table between them and turned to face her. "Should you base your current actions on something that happened almost ten years ago? You were both so young. Perhaps you should talk to him again."

"I had moved on, and until recently I was open to the addresses of other gentlemen. But he lingers on in my head. We had a pleasant meal together a few months ago and I invited him to dine with us when you and Darien were at Paradise, as you know. I was actually hopeful, fool that I am, and then he left abruptly that night. When I finally asked him why he told me he was just a farrier and intended to stay a farrier. He said that I was destined for great things and that he works for a living."

"That may be what he thinks, but what does he feel?"

That question plagued her as she fell asleep that night. She thought about how he had looked at her that night at Paradise as he left. He'd seemed as melancholy as she. Was it possible, or even imaginable, that he felt the same way about her as she did about him? Was he just shy? Or as unable to communicate as she was?

BY WEDNESDAY MORNING, OLIVIA HAD MADE A DECISION. SHE needed to get home. Mother's telegram on Monday had said Aunt Brigid was ill with a bad cough and aches and fever but that she was better for Eleanor being there. This morning's telegram said her aunt's condition was still the same. She knew she could do little more than her mother was already doing, but it didn't matter. It was Aunt Brigid who was ill, and she needed and wanted to be there. Arrangements were made for Olivia to catch the late afternoon train although she nearly didn't board.

"What do you mean she cannot go?" Josephine said to her housekeeper after conferring quietly with the woman in the hallway.

"Her father's had an accident and may not live through the day. I told her to go home to her mother immediately," the woman replied. "I didn't think there was anything else to do."

"There wasn't, Mrs. Emerson. You did the right thing. Thank you," Josephine said and turned to Olivia. "The maid who was to go with you is unable to. Perhaps you can wait until tomorrow for other arrangements to be made."

Olivia shook her head. "I'm certain I'll be fine. It's only a few hours until I get to Winchester, and then I'll have someone from Wilkins's Stables get me home. There's no need to fuss."

"There certainly is a need," Darien said. "I don't like the idea of a young woman traveling alone. Let alone the fact that your brother would ride here and shoot me between the eyes if anything happened to you. I promised to keep you safe."

"And I will be safe. The conductors on the trip here were attentive, and there's no reason to think they won't be the same on the trip home. You said you were able to get me a semiprivate car so I will be well looked after."

"I don't like it," he said.

"Could you speak to one of the conductors and ask him to keep a close eye on Olivia?" Josephine said to him.

"I suppose so. I suppose a few dollars toward his pocket couldn't hurt, either," he said. "As soon as I've seen you on the train, I will telegraph Paradise that you are on the way to them and begin to pray that nothing happens to you so I won't have to face Adam and Matthew and that other giant, Mr. Somerset."

Olivia kissed Josephine on both cheeks. "I have had a wonderful and most relaxing visit. What a lovely week it's been. Won't you come stay at Paradise for an extended visit? Mother and I would love to have you."

"I believe I will. Paradise is such a stark contrast to Washington, and yet I enjoyed those few days very much and wished I'd had more time."

"Come when the mares are foaling. It's a wonderful time, although I work in the barns most of the days. All of us do."

Josephine hugged her close and kissed her cheek. "Tell him, Olivia. You must tell him how you feel," she whispered.

THE CONDUCTOR SHOWED OLIVIA TO HER CAR, SETTING HER leather satchel beside her and asking if there was anything else she needed. Her trunk was stowed with the rest of the luggage, and she had her reticule in her lap. She could see Darien watching her through the window and waved to him. He waved back just as the train began to chug away. She leaned back and let her head fall against the window as she stared at the passing landscape.

Even if she decided to tell him how she felt, when would she do it? She couldn't very well walk up to him on the street and tell him she loved him. She smiled to herself imagining seeing him after church on a Sunday morning and saying, "Wasn't that a lovely sermon and by the way, I love you."

But her smile faded as she pictured his seventeen-year-old face telling her that he would never marry her. Maybe she would tell him the day she left to move to Washington. There would be no future awkwardness that way, no bad feelings between the families, and she would have given voice to what she'd been deeply burying for a decade. There would have to be something soothing in that alone, wouldn't there? To say it. To say the words and mean them with no expectations.

She loved him even knowing he would never love her. Maybe

this was the "sorting out" her mother had encouraged. Maybe she was fully mature enough to understand that loving someone never meant the beloved was obligated to return any regard. She loved him. Maybe that was enough. It would have to be.

She drifted off to sleep, lulled by the chug of the engine and the car's rhythmic swaying. She woke suddenly when she was thrown from her seat and on to her knees, slowly sliding to the wall under the window as the car she was in tilted. The older woman seated toward the back of the car was moaning, and a young person, a servant, she thought, was comforting her. Olivia could hear shouting and a screech and bangs as other cars slowed down, hitting the cars ahead of them, jarring her as she hung on to the edge of the seat. She pulled herself up to the window and looked outside. Snow was coming down steadily and she could already tell that there were several feet of it on the ground. She looked at the watch pinned to her dress under her coat and saw that two hours had passed since she'd left Washington. The door at the end of the car banged open and the conductor lurched in. He was holding a bloody handkerchief to his forehead.

"Is anyone hurt?" he shouted.

"I cannot move my leg." The older woman said one word at a time, punctuated by heavy breaths.

"It may be broken," the young woman with her said. "She won't let me help her."

"How could you help me? You are nothing but a housemaid!"

Olivia walked unsteadily to the conductor. "Where are we?"

"Outside of Harper's Ferry. We just crossed the bridge."

"What happened? Do you know?"

"We rounded a corner and ran into a snowdrift. Thank goodness we hadn't picked up speed after the crossing."

"Sit down," she said to the conductor. "Let me look at your head."

"I need help, right this instant! Don't you dare sit down!" the older woman said.

Olivia rummaged through her things until she found her white flannel nightgown. She loved that nightgown as it was warm and soft from many washings, but she tore the small hem with her teeth and ripped a strip from the bottom. "Sit," she said to the conductor. "You cannot help anyone else if you need help yourself. Let me see this cut."

Olivia threw the blood-soaked handkerchief to the floor. "The cut is not deep, but wounds to the head tend to—" She quickly grabbed the back of the bench beside her as the train car lurched forward.

The older woman screamed, and the young girl with her began to cry. Olivia made her way to them. "You must stop shouting," she said and turned to the young woman when the older one quieted. "I will help you in a moment. Are you able to stand?"

"Yes, ma'am."

Olivia turned back to the conductor and dabbed the cut. She made a padding with a piece of her nightgown and tied it tightly about his head with a long strip of fabric.

"You are as calm a young lady as I've ever met, miss," he said. "I was told to keep watch over you, and here you are taking care of me."

"Don't worry a bit, sir. I want you to be able to attend to passengers in other cars. I'm guessing we'll be walking back to Harper's Ferry before soon or it will be very, very cold overnight," she said quietly.

He nodded and whispered, "Yes, miss. I don't imagine there'll be another way."

Olivia knotted off the bandage. "Let me get this older lady settled and then I will come with you to see if I can help any others." She knelt down beside the older woman, who was now sniffling and red-faced. "Ma'am? Ma'am?"

"See here, young woman. I need attention immediately. When will assistance arrive?"

"Help will arrive, but it may be too long to wait. We must help ourselves. Your young woman and I are going to help you onto the bench."

"Do not touch me!"

"Ma'am," Olivia said forcefully. "You must listen to me. You are frightened and maybe hurt. There is no time for dramatics. Now lean forward so I can help you up or let me examine your leg."

The woman was red-faced and clearly agitated but her bottom lip was trembling wildly. She huffed out a breath. "There is a man in the room!"

Olivia glanced at the conductor. "Please step outside for just a moment, sir."

"This is outrageous!" the woman said haughtily.

"Please settle down. I'm sure there are others that have been hurt worse than you, and I am going to help them immediately if you won't allow me to ascertain your injuries."

"Go ahead. See what you can see then! I've never been so dissatisfied in all of my life! My husband knows the owners of the Washington & Atlantic and they will hear about this!"

Olivia lifted the woman's skirts and petticoats. "You landed awkwardly on your leg when you fell. Can you straighten out if I help you?"

"It is feeling numb," the woman said.

"Most likely because you have cut off the circulation to your limb." Olivia gently pulled the woman's leg out in front of her. She felt up and down both of her legs but could feel no breaks, and the woman didn't shout or faint, which she surely would have done if there was a broken bone.

Olivia and the servant helped the woman up to the bench. "Move your foot around and try to get the blood flowing," she said. "I am Miss Olivia Gentry, ma'am, from Winchester."

"I am Mrs. Frederick Lehrner of the Philadelphia Lehrners."

"It is a pleasure to meet you," she said and turned to the young woman. "Find you and your mistress some shawls in your bags, or there may be some blankets in that chest attached to the wall there. It will be cold in here soon. I'm going with the conductor to help other passengers, but I will make sure someone attends you as soon as possible."

Olivia pulled on her coat and took a moment to add a pair of heavy wool socks over her thin stockings. She replaced her boots, lacing them tightly, and wrapped a scarf around her neck. She pulled open the door at the end of the car.

"Where shall we begin?" she asked the conductor. "I'm Olivia Gentry, sir."

The conductor nodded. "Owen McMaster, Miss Gentry. The porters and coal men and the engineer are going car to car as we speak. There's no need for you to do anything but shelter in your car until we begin moving passengers."

"There is need everywhere, I imagine, Mr. McMaster. We are wasting time talking, are we not?"

McMaster blew out a breath. "Yes, miss. Follow me then and be careful of the last step. The snow is deep."

CHAPTER 13

"Wake up, Jim!" he heard after the pounding on his door stopped. He sat up, shook his head to clear his deep sleep, and pulled open the door.

"Good Lord, Phillip, quit your screaming," he said and yanked his brother into the room and out of the blowing snow. "What?" he said, suddenly panicked. "Is there a fire? Is someone ill?"

"No," he said and took a gulp of air. "Mrs. Gentry is here. Mother wants you right away."

"Mrs. Gentry? What time is it?" He picked up his pocket watch from the nightstand. "It's three in the morning!"

"You'd better hurry!" Phillip said as he went back out into the night.

Jim went up the back steps of the house moments later and directly into the kitchen, where he could see lamps lit. Mrs. Gentry and his mother were seated at the kitchen table, each holding a cup of something steaming. Emmaline was leaning against the stove, Phillip under her arm, while Helen put cookies on a plate. Everyone was in their nightclothes except Eleanor Gentry. His mother stood quickly when he came through the door.

"Oh, Jim. You must hurry. Go back immediately and dress as warmly as you can. You must hurry," she said as she wrung her handkerchief.

Emmaline put her arm around her mother and seated her. "Let Mrs. Gentry explain things, Mother. You are overexcited."

He looked at Olivia's mother. She'd always been a bit aloof, but that wasn't the right word he thought, because she'd been as kind and loving a mother as his own and was as good to him as she was to Matthew or Adam when he was a young boy and visiting Paradise. She was always in command, even though Mr. Gentry was loud and often barking orders and jokes and laughing in his booming voice. It was to her, though, that everyone turned when a final decision was to be made. He'd seen it happen. But tonight, she was white-faced and her eyes, always focused on her listener and smiling, were worried.

"Mrs. Gentry," he said as she stood. "What can I do for you?"

"It's Olivia, Jim. You must go for her."

"Go for her? In Washington? Has something happened?"

"She was on her way home, and her train derailed near Harper's Ferry. Thank God they got across the river."

"You've heard from her?" he asked.

She shook her head. "No. I received a telegram from Matthew's friend, Darien, that she'd boarded the train to come home yesterday. Mr. Witherspoon got the telegram to me around eight in the evening. He was delayed for some reason. I didn't know what to do or think, knowing she should have been home hours earlier, but then not long ago there was a pounding at my door. He returned saying he had an emergency telegraph for the Winchester train stationmaster that the Washington & Atlantic afternoon train had derailed and to let anyone know who might be expecting passengers. He hurried back to tell me."

Jim looked down at his hands now holding Eleanor Gentry's shaking ones. His mind was piecing together what she'd said, and he couldn't stop the rising terror and hysteria he felt. Olivia could be dead. She could be gone to her reward this very moment.

"I refuse to think the worst, Jim. I refuse, and you must as well."

He would pray, he thought. He would fall on his knees and pray that she was safe, seeing her in his mind's eye, young and vibrant and beautiful. He didn't know if he would survive if she were gone. And then he realized Mrs. Gentry was still talking to him.

"I hate to ask this of you but . . ."

"Jim! Hurry! Get changed!" his mother urged.

He squeezed Mrs. Gentry's hands. "I'm sorry. I didn't hear what you need me to do."

"Adam and Matthew are gone to Bridgewater for the sale of Annie's house. I was going to send George, and he is willing to go, but he is ill with the same thing as Aunt Brigid. I cannot send Ben. I don't . . ."

"Phillip," he said and turned. "Saddle Jasper. Do not worry, Mrs. Gentry. I'll go for her."

Mrs. Gentry stopped Phillip at the door with her hand on his shoulder. "I've ridden one of the Morgans here. York. Take him."

"You rode here in the middle of the night?" he asked.

"I had to climb up the side of stall to get him saddled. He's seventeen hands and will be able to handle your weight and hers, too, if you must . . . bring her home."

"I know York. He's the pride of Paradise. Are you sure you want me to take him?"

"Her father would insist on it."

"Stay here, Mrs. Gentry, until someone can get you to Paradise. Phillip, get to Wilkins's Stables at first light and arrange a carriage for Mrs. Gentry and then park yourself at the telegraph office. I will let you know I have arrived at Harper's Ferry and what I've found out about Olivia. You're welcome, I'm sure, to stay here with Mother, Mrs. Gentry. Then you would hear any news quickly."

"Oh, yes, Eleanor. Stay here. We'll get a message to your aunt that you're with us," his mother said.

Jim hurried to his room and pulled on two layers of clothing and his heavy coat lined with sheep's wool. He gathered some supplies for his saddlebags and rolled up blankets. He checked York's saddle and bridle and went into the kitchen to let them know he was going.

"I'm leaving," he said as the wind swept in the kitchen behind him.

"Here are sandwiches and cheese. Do you have a canteen?" his mother asked, and he nodded.

He kissed her cheek and looked at Phillip. "You know what you are to do?"

"Yes, sir."

Eleanor Gentry stood. "Thank you. Thank you. I didn't know who else to ask."

"Be easy, Mrs. Gentry. Adam or Matthew would do the same for my mother. I'll take the same care as I would with my own sisters."

He heard Emmaline harrumph and went out the door.

* * *

OLIVIA WAS CRADLING AN INFANT AND HOLDING THE HAND OF a toddler, trudging through the snow close to dawn. She was on her second trip walking to the town of Harper's Ferry. The town itself she discovered when there but an hour ago was still not rebuilt completely from the years of the war. The townspeople had rallied to help the passengers, but it wasn't a place large enough to help them all, even with citizens opening their homes and businesses supplying what was needed. She'd made the first trip behind the cart that had been brought out for the injured, although thankfully there were very few. Mrs. Lehrner had insisted on riding alone in the cart until Olivia threatened to have her removed bodily if she did not stop shouting and move over to make room for an elderly couple.

Her wool dress was soaked, ice crusted up to her knees, and her feet were so cold she could hardly feel them. She didn't know if she could make another trip. She was exhausted. But then she looked around at the older persons and young ones still on the train, now shivering with cold, waiting their turn to be helped as they wouldn't be able to navigate through the deep snow. She was young and healthy, tired to be sure right now, but she was not feeble and knew her duty. The steep incline to her right, where the ground had been carved out of the hill for the train tracks gave way to a field with frozen half stalks of corn, began to lessen. She would soon be able to see the lights of Harper's Ferry ahead. She looked up when she heard shouting.

"Olivia!"

"Jim?" she shouted and scanned the ridge. "Jim? Is that you?"

Was that York he'd just jumped down from? He was hurrying to her, picking his way quickly until he came near her, but five or so feet above her. He slipped and slid his way down until he was beside her.

He stared at her, took a deep breath, and closed his eyes.

"I am so glad you're here! Is that York you're riding? Do you think you can get this child in front of you and into town? She's freezing in her thin dress," she said.

His eyes flew open. "I'll carry you to York. Give the child to her mother."

"Jim! Her mother is already in town. We couldn't take all of her children at once. These two stayed with their father, who has a head injury and is being helped by the conductor. I promised I would get them to her."

He had ridden York as fast and hard as he could through fields, and on some roads, trying to get to her as quickly as he could. He wanted to kiss her. He wanted to hold her until his heart slowed its gallop. He wanted to pick her up and carry her away. He looked up and down the line of people now stopped from trudging through the snow as he and Olivia talked.

"Of course. Give me the child and the other one, too. I can hold them both," he said as he squeezed past others and climbed the bank to York only a few feet above where they walked. "I'll be back shortly. Town is close by. Where am I taking the children?"

"To the saloon. Their mother's name is Mary."

Jim kneed York once he was settled on the horse's back and a man had handed him up the children. He opened his coat and put them inside. Both were sniffling and crying. He rode slowly as he wrestled with the older child as she bucked and kicked him. He talked softly to her in the same voice he'd used when his younger siblings were upset or frightened. But this child would not settle down, and he imagined she thought she was fighting for her life.

He found the saloon and deposited the children with the frantic mother, who fell to her knees kissing her children and crying. There was an older woman he could hear screeching that she would be informing the owners of the railroad that she had been taken to a *saloon* over the quiet talk of the rest of the train passengers spread out at the tables and at the stand-up bar. He found the telegraph office but the desk was empty with just a note saying the operator was out helping passengers. Jim found paper and pencil and wrote. "Olivia alive and well. Will bring her home as soon as able." He left the note on the desk with a gold piece and another note asking to send his message to Eleanor Gentry of Paradise at the Winchester office immediately.

JIM RODE YORK AS FAST AS HE DARED THROUGH ROUGH FIELDS to get back to Olivia. He found her comforting an expectant mother. She was tearing fabric and making a bandage with it to wrap the arm of the young man with the woman and a young child.

"I am so glad you have come back so quickly. Can we get Mrs. McMinn on York? She is exhausted, and Mr. McMinn's arm is cut from broken glass. I cannot stop the bleeding and have nothing to stitch the wound with," she said and looked from his face to the young man's bandage as it slowly turned red.

"She cannot ride up there alone. I'll ride and hold her in front of me. Can you get the father to the saloon? You're not too far, and I'll come back as soon as I've deposited them," he said.

"Of course. York can hold you both. It's a short distance you say? Good. Then hurry back. There is an elderly man who will not accept help and I'm worried he is getting too cold."

Jim stared at her as she consoled people trudging past her and helped a young man with a bandage about his feet. Her nose was shining and her hair was down around her face. Her dress was solid ice from her knees to its hem and her hands were cherry red. She was directing those around her, having clearly taken charge in a dreadful situation, much as her brothers and mother would do, he thought. There was nothing silly or immature or ridiculous about her as there was occasionally about his sisters and others back in Winchester. She could have led a regiment in the War between the States and been as successful as Grant. She was formidable.

"Jim? Can you take Mrs. McMinn?"

He pulled himself up into the saddle and maneuvered York to a slight gully in the snow. "Here, ma'am. Give me your arms and I will lift you up."

The woman was crying, and her child was, too, as Olivia bent to comfort her and tell her she would be fine even though York's back seemed very, very far away. The young man was telling his wife to be careful and that he loved her. Jim bent over as far as he could and lifted the woman to sit in front of him. He slid over the back of the saddle and sat the woman sideways behind the horn and reached for the child. He settled them both and gave York a nudge.

Two hours later everyone was in the town somewhere, in someone's home or on the floor of the saloon. Some of the men in the stables, or in the back of the general store.

"I can't thank you enough, Miss Gentry," the weary conductor said as they walked into Harper's Ferry.

"No more than anyone would do, Mr. McMaster," she said. "I was glad to be able to help, especially the children and their mothers who were so frightened."

"Not everyone would have done what you did, or what your friend here did. My thanks to you, and I intend to tell my superiors we were fortunate to have you on board. Where will you be staying? You must get some sleep and out of those wet clothes before you catch your death. It may be a day or so until we can shovel the tracks enough to continue, but we'll be getting to the trunks in the baggage car as soon as we've rested and warmed up."

"I don't know where we'll be staying," she said, "but I'm sure we'll find a space somewhere. Get some rest yourself. I've been told the women from the church down the street have cooked up meals and drinks."

"I'll do that, miss. And thank you again."

Jim watched the conductor walk away and turned to Olivia. She looked up at him with wide eyes.

"I couldn't believe it when I saw you on York standing on that ridge. How did you find me? How did you know?"

"Let's get you warm and dry and then we'll talk."

She looked up and down the street. "I guess we could go in the saloon."

"I got the last room at the boardinghouse down at the end of town when I brought those children to their mother. It's the attic room, barely used, and the woman said there's some storage in there but said she'd have hot wash water brought up for you and light the fireplace so you can get warm."

"Oh, to be warm," she said and closed her eyes, swaying as she stood.

"How long have you been out here?" he asked as they went down the muddy street toward the boarding house.

"I don't know. I think I made three trips from the train to town. I think. I'm so tired, my mind's a muddle."

OLIVIA FELT AS THOUGH ALL THE EFFORTS SHE'D MADE IN THE last six or seven hours were bearing down on her at that very moment when she was no longer thinking of anyone else but herself and her own situation. Her teeth were chattering, and she felt as if each step took every bit of her energy and concentration. She stumbled over a mound of dirt or manure, and Jim caught her to his side and then picked her up in his arms.

"What are you doing?" she asked even as she laid her head on his shoulder.

"Don't start fussing."

"I'm not fussing. I can walk. You don't have to carry me."

"Shush, now. We're almost there."

She gave in with a sigh. It felt very good to be in someone's arms, especially if that someone was Jim Somerset. He wasn't breathing hard, even carrying her down the street and up on to the stoop of the boardinghouse. The door opened and he turned sideways to get inside. The warmth hit her face and made the skin on her cheeks itch.

"Get her up the steps, young man," an older woman was saying. "I heard this is the young lady who has helped so many passengers. I've got my grandsons carrying warm water and the hip bath. Two flights. Keep going now."

Olivia let herself relax against him and rubbed her nose on the soft lamb's wool on the collar of his coat. She closed her eyes and took a deep breath of pine trees and cold air and man. It was Jim holding her, and she realized if she'd ever need rescuing, which perhaps she did right this moment, then this was the man she wanted to save her. She smiled to herself thinking of that.

"Here. I'll get the door. I've got the fireplace going good and put some clean sheets on the bed. There's extra quilts on the dresser there. Is your wife hungry?"

"She's not—"

"Yes. I'm starved and thirsty. Thank you so much for accommodating us," Olivia said.

"I'll bring tea and soup I made just today. And some bread. I suppose you're hungry, too," the woman said and looked at Jim as he sat Olivia down on the bed. "But you'll need more than soup."

Jim turned to the woman. "Can you help her off with her clothes and such? I've got to get my horse stabled."

"Of course," she said. "You hurry along. I've got a nightgown here for her. We'll get her all fixed up."

Olivia watched the woman's grandsons haul water to the copper tub sitting in front of the fire. She shivered as her clothes began to melt, dripping cold water down the back of her legs. She let the woman pull off her coat and shake it and undo the buttons on her blouse. She stood at the woman's urging.

"I'm Mrs. Johnson, by the way," she said as she unbuttoned Olivia's skirts and heavy petticoats. They fell to the floor in a soggy mess.

"Olivia . . . Somerset," she said and looked up as the woman stared at her. "We've not been married long and sometimes I forget my new name."

Mrs. Johnson smiled. "Newlyweds, huh? I could tell, with him carrying you down the street."

Olivia smiled and let the woman undo her corset and pull her silk chemise over her head. She tried to undo her garters herself, but her fingers wouldn't cooperate. Mrs. Johnson pushed her hands away.

"Let me, dear," she said. "Your hands are so cold they're near frozen."

She sat as the woman undid the laces on her boots and sat them in front of the fire. She rolled down her cotton stockings and put them in the pile with the rest of Olivia's clothes.

"I'm going to get your clothes clean and dry. You get yourself in the warm water," Mrs. Johnson said. "I didn't make it too hot. Not until you're warmed up a bit. There's soap there, too, on the little table. Can you reach it?"

Olivia walked to the tub and put a foot in. It made her skin tingle but felt heavenly. "Oh," she groaned as she sank down into the water, dunking her head as she went. "This feels so wonderful."

"I'll be back with some food and drink and see if you need anything else. I'm thinking a nice long nap when your husband gets back would be the best medicine for you," Mrs. Johnson said with a wink.

Olivia soaped her hair and dipped her head. The steam smelled like lavender, and the fireplace was crackling and sparking as she leaned back against the tub. Her muscles were aching from all the walking and hauling she'd done, and she worried she'd drop off to sleep in the water if she wasn't careful. She stretched her legs and yawned.

"Come in, Mrs. Johnson," she said to the knock on the door. The woman bustled in carrying a tray covered with a cloth.

"Let me help you get out and into this warm nightgown I've had hanging near the fireplace."

Olivia stepped out of the tub and dried off. Mrs. Johnson pulled the nightgown over her head, and she sat down in the rocker in front of the fire. The grandsons came back into the room and hauled away the water and the tub and brought a clean basin of water and rags and sat them on the dry sink.

Mrs. Johnson closed the door as Olivia rubbed her hair with a dry towel in front of the fire. She picked up the bowl of beef soup and sipped slowly. She didn't think she'd ever been so tired in her life. She took a few sips of tea, pulled a quilt tightly around her, and stared into the fire.

"Livie?" she heard from the hallway.

"Come in, Jim."

"There's a chair downstairs I can sit in."

She opened the door, holding the quilt around herself. "Come inside. I want to hear how you found me. Mother must be frantic! I just thought of it."

"I sent a telegraph on my first trip to town."

He was still standing outside her door, twirling his hat, although he was in his stocking feet.

"Come inside. It's cold in the hallway."

"I don't think so. I mean I shouldn't. I don't . . . I can't do it."

"You can't cross this threshold?" she said with a small smile. "It's surely not too high to lift your foot over."

He shook his head. "No. That's not it, Livie. You know it's not."

"Please?"

She watched him swallow with closed eyes. When he opened them he walked into the room, nearly touching the ceiling with his head. She backed up to the bed and sat down, pulling the quilt tighter around her.

"You must be exhausted, too," she said. "Sit down before you fall down and tell me how you got here."

He sat down in the rocker in front of the fire. It squeaked with his weight as he settled. He held his feet up to the fire and then leaned forward to warm his hands. He told her about her mother and the telegraphs from Washington.

"I never meant to worry anyone," she said and shook her head. "I just wanted to get home to Aunt Brigid. She's ill."

"I know. My mother told me that your mother came home early and that you stayed in Washington." He stared at her.

She nodded and looked at her toes peeking out from under the voluminous nightgown she wore. "I did."

"Are you moving there?"

"I don't know. I don't know what to think."

The room was silent other than the crackling of the logs in the fireplace until Jim stood, sending the rocker skittering away. He stood staring at her from the side of the bed, his knees touching the mattress, breathing heavily and clenching his fists. This was it, she thought. This was when she would put herself out there and see if something said a decade ago still mattered. Whether she could take one more minute in the small room and not touch him. She knelt on the bed, and inched toward him. She reached up and pulled his head down with shaking hands and a wish.

She pressed her lips to his softly, breathing in the scent of him, and feeling the rough rasp of his whiskers against her palms. He was shaking as much as she was. She broke the kiss and stared at him, inches from his face.

"You told me you could never care for me, but sometimes it seems that you do."

"I never said that."

"Yes, you did. You told me when I was fifteen."

He shook his head. "You're Matt's sister. I couldn't say—"

"Won't you tell me what you're feeling?"

He licked his lips, never taking his eyes from her. "I'm terrified."

"You're frightened of me?"

"No," he said and touched her cheek with a shaking hand. "I'm terrified that if something begins here, I'll not be able to stop myself."

"What if I don't want you to stop?"

"You're destined for great things, Livie," he said.

She stared at his mouth and then looked up into his eyes. "What if I'm destined for you?"

He shook his head and started to speak, but she stopped him with her mouth on his. She could feel his ragged breath against her lips. And suddenly she was in his arms. His mouth covered hers with a moan.

He touched the seam of her mouth with his tongue and she went limp, barely holding on to his arms. He laid her back on the bed, put one knee beside her, and leaned over.

"If I . . . I won't be able to stop," he whispered.

"I'm saying yes."

She grabbed him by the collar and pulled his face down to hers. And then the rhythm changed from hers to his. He stretched out beside her and leaned over to cover her, kissing her mouth, her eyes, and her hair as he ran an arm under her neck, pulling her toward him. She could feel his urgency in the weight of his hands and reveled in it. She kissed him back and touched his chest where his shirt was open.

He kissed her openmouthed, moving his tongue in and out of hers, making her hips roll up to his. She put her hand on his backside and pulled him tightly against her. She was frustrated that she was not able to touch warm skin and began to unbutton his shirt. He sat up and pulled it over his head. She couldn't take her eyes from his chest, dark hair thick in the center and narrowing to a point at the waist of his heavy pants. She knelt up on the bed and pulled the nightgown over her head.

"Jesus," he whispered, staring at her, and stood, tearing at the buttons on his pants and hopping on each foot to pull off thick socks. "Jesus."

She could feel the tips of her breasts harden as he looked at her. She didn't feel shy or embarrassed. She could only feel this was her fate, her destiny, her chance to feel what she'd only dreamed about. Being in his arms.

She was on her back in the next moment, the bed creaking as he came down on top of her. She could feel the hard length of his erection against her stomach. It made her squirm under him.

"Please," she said reveling in the feel of his long and muscled legs against her, his chest against her breasts.

"I've never done this, Olivia. I've been waiting."

"Waiting for what?" she whispered.

"For this moment. I've been waiting for you."

"I thought you didn't . . ." she began and shook her head. "Touch me, please, Jim."

He kissed her and ran a hand down her side, stopping at her breast, weighing it in his palm, and running his thumb over her nipple. He lifted his head to stare into her eyes. She arched her back and pressed into his hand.

"Does this feel good, Livie?"

"Oh, please."

"I want to touch you," he said and swallowed and looked down the length of her body. "I've dreamed about touching you there."

She opened her legs to him, feeling the rough hair of his leg as she ran her toes up his shin. "Touch me then."

He groaned and ran his hand down her body, over her stomach with feather weight traces and into the curls at the juncture of her thighs, tickling the sensitive center of her. Her hips jerked. She drew in a sharp breath as he ran a finger where he had parted her. She was wet, and he was panting as he watched his hand make circles until he dipped a finger into her.

He climbed over her then, quickly spreading her legs with his knees and bringing his sex to hers. He was above her, his arms straight and massive and muscular. She ran her fingers over his chest and tilted her hips to him.

"I'm going to hurt you, Livie. I don't want to, but I think it always happens," he said, shaking his head and looking at her worriedly.

"I've been waiting for this moment, too. Forever it seems," She lifted her hips and rubbed herself against the tip of him.

He came down on his forearms, trapping her, covering her, rubbing his chest against hers, as he began to move inside of her. She was feeling full of him when he made one hard thrust, joining them completely. It took her a moment to get used to the shock of it, to the strangeness of him inside her, until she relaxed as he kissed her face and hair and murmured in her ear.

His hips pulled out and in again against hers in a slow grind. She could hear the wetness and feel his entry with each stroke. She lifted herself to him, panting, as he sped up, his face intense and concentrated on her. Her tongue touched her lips, and he thrust into her hard and fast, groaning and straining. Her eyes closed and she felt light and out of touch with where she was, out of her body but fused with his, until his weight descended on her and she wrapped her arms around him.

CHAPTER 14

Jim's eyes opened and he stared at the ceiling above him. It took a long minute to remember where he was. He looked down at Olivia, sleeping soundly, her head on his shoulder, her hand splayed across his bare chest. She was naked and warm, and he could feel the weight and shape of her breast against his side. It was intensely erotic, he thought, as he watched the sheet covering him begin to tent. He'd had intercourse with Olivia Gentry. He'd seen her magnificent body unclothed. He'd touched her intimately, and she'd touched him. He'd made love to her.

But his thoughts were interrupted by a voice in the back of his head, shouting at him, shouting out in anger, and recalling all the rage he'd felt as he rode on York in the dead and cold of the night, all the terror and prayers that had drifted through his mind thinking of her body twisted and broken in a train wreck's aftermath. Was she still moving to Washington? To find weighty conversation and more sophisticated company than Winchester could ever offer? He was furious then, breathing harshly, thinking about her plans as she shifted and laid a long leg over his.

He sat up abruptly, feeling sordid, and disloyal to a family, to men he'd known all of his life. She tumbled onto her stomach and lifted her head from the pillow, her hair shadowing her face. She pushed the strands out of the way and smiled at him.

"Hello," she said. "What time is it?"

He stood and pulled on his pants. He looked back over his shoulder at her. "Time to go."

"What is it?" she whispered.

He turned and looked at her sitting there, staring up at him wide-eyed and lovely and virginal and everything single thing he'd ever dreamed of. Naked and warm and ready for him again, he could it see it in her shy smile and the slow blink of her long lashes. He felt horribly guilty and angry, and unhappy to have to deal with the tumult of emotions he was feeling.

"We've got a long ride ahead of us," he said and pulled on his shirt.

"Jim. What is it? What have I done?"

He righted the rocker, sat down, and pulled on his wool socks. "Done? Just worried everyone to death. That's all."

"Why are you so angry now? You weren't angry last night."

"Why do you care, Olivia? You'll be gone from Winchester and not have to concern yourself with me."

Even as he said the words, even as he watched her smile fade, her shoulders drop, even as she reeled back from his words, covering her mouth with her hand, he couldn't help himself. If he gave in now, kissed her and loved her again, he'd be lost forever, worshipping her and losing himself in the process, as she merrily tripped away to the next thing that caught her attention. She swallowed visibly.

"Jim," she whispered as tears rolled down her cheeks. "How could you think—"

"I'm sure there will be someone to take my place when you're settled in Washington." He stood and pulled on his coat. "I'll arrange for your trunk to be delivered to the Winchester station when they finally get this train moving. We'll take York and be back home faster. Is half an hour enough time for you to be ready?"

He opened the door and stared into the hallway waiting for her reply. He hated his weakness. She was his everything. Didn't she know that?

"I'll be ready."

OLIVIA GAVE IN AND LEANED BACK AGAINST THE SOLID WALL OF his chest, after having sat upright and away from him for the first hour they were on York's back as she was too angry, too crushed to do anything else for as long as she could manage. She couldn't reconcile the man who'd made love to her with the man behind her, his arms around her, loosely holding York's reins in his hands. He managed the massive horse with little more than the slight movement of his fingers or the tap of his knees.

She was reminded of riding in front of her father when she was a young girl. Tears threatened again as she thought of how much she missed him and how much she wished she could throw herself in her daddy's arms and tell him all of her problems. He would solve it for her, she was certain of that.

"We'll be coming to Paradise first," he said. "I'll leave York and take another horse home and have Phillip return him."

She said nothing. She didn't trust herself to talk to him even about the most mundane of subjects. But she had come to some conclusions on their ride and knew she must deal with the truth rather than hide behind some false modesty. She'd lost her virginity the night before. She loved Jim Somerset. She was leaving Winchester for good.

Paradise came into sight from the northern ridge and she barely restrained herself from jumping down and walking the rest of the way. York trotted onto the shelled drive as her mother came out of the house. She awkwardly slung her leg and skirts over the horse's neck and slid down his side. Her mother gathered her in her arms.

Olivia buried her face in her mother's shoulder and breathed deeply of home. She allowed herself to be petted and kissed until she was able to look her mother in the eye and smile wanly.

"Jim," Eleanor said and walked to him as he dismounted from York and handed off the reins to George. "I can never thank you enough for what you've done."

Olivia heard him reply and walked toward the house, seeing Aunt Brigid and Ben in the doorway. Her mother called to her that Jim was leaving, but she didn't raise a hand or turn her head. Whatever had begun all those tormented years ago, that had shriveled with disappointment and flared bright with hope on occasion, was now dead. It was finished. She wouldn't turn back.

* * *

"COME IN," OLIVIA SAID TO THE KNOCK ON HER BEDROOM door the following day. "Good morning, Mother."

"Writing a letter, dear?"

"Yes," she said and turned from her desk chair to smile at her mother, who was seating herself on the bed. "I'm writing to Josephine and Darien."

"Ah," she said. "I've yet to send a thank-you letter. I must do so without delay."

Olivia blew on the paper and folded it. "I've asked Darien to begin a search for a town house for me to purchase or rent. I'd like to be settled there by spring."

"You've decided definitely to go, then," Eleanor said some moments later.

She stood and walked to her mother. She picked up her hands and clasped them tightly. "Yes, I have. It's high time I begin my own life, and I liked Washington. It's good to know I'll have a friend or two in my new hometown."

"What happened between you and Jim?"

"Nothing, Mother," she said and shook her head. "Nothing at all."

"You didn't even speak to him when he left. He'd traveled quite a distance in the middle of the night at my behest. He brought you home to us. He looked terribly upset as he rode away, so strange for the Jim I know who is always even-tempered and—"

"Leave it, Mother," she said gently. "There is nothing more to say."

Eleanor searched her eyes. "Love always has something to say. Sometimes it shouts from the highest hill, and sometimes it whispers so softly one must listen closely to hear. Do not turn away, Olivia. It is a rare and precious commodity. Treasure it." Eleanor touched her cheek and smiled. "But you are right. You're an adult woman in an exciting new world. Find what it is you need to find."

"I intend to," she said. "I'm looking forward to it."

Eleanor stood. "Adam is home, and Matt and Annie are coming here for the noonday meal. I've had Mabel make a special dinner for their homecoming and yours."

ADAM WRAPPED HER IN A HUG WHEN SHE CAME DOWN THE steps and kissed her forehead. "Come. Matt and Annie are already in the dining room."

Annie hugged her tightly, and Matt looked at her with a laugh after kissing her cheek. "Why do I get the feeling there's more to this story than the train stopping in a snowdrift and you riding home up in front of Jim?"

She smiled as everyone was seated and Mabel and Beatrice brought platters to the table. "Well. There was an odious woman in the semiprivate car with me." She held her nose and spoke. "Mrs. Frederick Lehrner of the Philadelphia Lehrners! 'I am acquainted with the owners of this railroad and they will hear about my dissatisfaction!'"

Everyone laughed and she continued on, telling them about falling out of her seat, patching up the conductor's cut, and making all the trips walking back and forth, carrying children and helping the elderly.

"I was near frozen when I heard Jim's voice," she said and finally looked up at her family. None of them were eating, although Matt still held his silverware in his hand. They were all staring at her.

"How long were you out in the cold, Livie?" Adam asked.

"Hours. There were a lot of cars and it was a very full train. So many children. The snow was far too deep at first and then treacherous after the first three or four groups tramped it down. There was a man who needed stitches desperately where he'd cut himself on a broken window. How I wished I'd packed my kit in my satchel instead of in my trunk, which I couldn't get to."

"How long, Livie?" Matt asked quietly.

She shrugged. "Most of the night, until we got everyone into the stables or the saloon or the general store."

"We?" Annie asked.

"The conductor and the train men, and Jim, of course."

"Well," her mother said. "It sounds as though you did your duty and more, dear."

"I was exhausted and cold and my clothes were so heavy with snow and ice they were dragging around my ankles. I was very glad Jim arranged for the last room at the boardinghouse for us. For me," she corrected. She looked down at her plate as she felt her face redden.

"For Jim and you," Adam repeated.

"The landlady was very kind. She brought me a warm bath and food and had my clothes ready for me when it was time to leave," she said.

"When was that?" Matt asked. "What time did you get on the road?"

Olivia looked at her brother, who was staring at her intently. It was never pleasant to be a subject of Matt's scrutiny when he was unsmiling and serious.

"I don't know exactly."

"Were you able to get any sleep?"

She swallowed and took a sip of tea. "Yes. Some."

"You are so brave and wonderful," Annie said with a glance around the table. "You could have lost your toes or fingers to the cold, but I'm guessing that would have still not stopped you from doing all that you could do."

Olivia smiled at her sister-in-law, grateful for the change of subject. "Tell me what happened with the sale of Annie's property."

Adam stared at her for a few more moments and picked up his knife and fork. "It was as routine as one could expect, and no one tried to kill us this time."

"Thank goodness," Annie said. "I'm just glad to be done with it all even if I do still miss my neighbors and the friends I had there."

"Maybe we'll visit after the foaling this spring," Matt said. "Would you like that?"

Olivia watched them smile at each other and Annie touch her brother's arm. Her mother was right. Love was precious. She was glad these two dear people were so happy and in love. After the meal was over, Adam and Matt went outside to the barns, and Eleanor to the kitchens to plan the following week's meals. Olivia went up to her room, and Annie followed, carrying Teddy.

"May we come in?" Annie asked when they came to Olivia's door.

"Of course," she said and took her nephew in her arms. "You are so sweet and such a big boy!" Teddy grabbed at her earbobs, and she sat down on the floor with him as he examined the blocks she'd pulled from the trunk near her bed.

"Mother says you are planning to move to Washington. That you've decided for sure," Annie said. "I'm going to miss you so much!"

"I'm going to miss you, too, and Teddy, and well, everyone," she said, looking down at the little boy.

"It will be very exciting, I imagine."

Olivia smiled. "Oh, yes. Washington is a very busy town and there are so many things to do and see. You'll have to come visit as soon as I'm settled in a house."

She looked up to see Annie staring at her.

"If there is something you'd like to talk about, maybe something you don't want to tell Mother, you know you can tell me. I'd never repeat a word of it."

"Why would you think there would be something I couldn't tell Mother?" Olivia asked and turned a block over in her hand. "What could there possibly be?"

But she knew she wasn't fooling Annie and was very close to tears. She stood and walked to the window, staring out into the deep woods, now brown and gray and white with snow on the branches. It had occurred to her the night before as she lay in her bed that she would most likely never have children. How could she ever marry someone other than him? She couldn't. She wouldn't. Even if it weren't cruel and dishonest to marry someone she could never love, she believed it was beyond her ability to go to a husband who would be expecting a virgin bride when she no longer was one. But more than that, more than any of it, how could she ever be intimate with someone other than Jim Somerset? She didn't think she could stomach it.

"We made love," she whispered. "I . . . I had no idea how I'd feel."

"What happened, Livie?"

She turned and smiled. "We slept for a few hours . . . after wards and he wasn't the same man suddenly. He told me he was sure I'd find someone to take his place in Washington."

Annie slumped. "Oh, Livie. How cruel! But why would he still think you were moving there?"

"I don't know," she said and shook her head. "How could he think I would want someone other than him after what we'd done together?"

"Men just aren't good at this," Annie said and shook her head. "I think Jim Somerset has been in love with you all of his life. Maybe he was hurt and lashing out at you. Oh, I don't know."

"If he'd said anything, anything that would have led me to think he was in love with me or cared for me, I would stay and see where it would all lead, but he didn't. He was so angry with me, and I have no idea why."

"Have you told him you love him?"

Olivia shook her head. "I never did. I will have that as a regret, I imagine."

"When Matt left me in Bridgewater, well, when I refused to go with him, I would sit and pray that one day I would stop thinking about him and that I'd told him how I felt about him. That he was the only man I'd ever love. I nearly drove myself insane thinking about it. You have time to make it right. Don't waste your chance."

JIM STOPPED TO WIPE HIS FACE. HE'D BEEN BENT OVER, bending shoes, working the forge for most of the day, trying to stop seeing Olivia's naked body in his mind's eye and to stop thinking about the look on her face as he'd told her to find someone new in Washington. There'd been nothing in his experience to prepare him for how he'd felt when she'd looked up at him with those perfect green eyes, stricken and hurt, the blood draining from her face leaving her skin ashen and translucent. How could he have said what he did?

But how could he have not? She was leaving him, leaving Paradise, her family's stake, her nephew and brothers and mother. How could she do it?

"Hello, Mr. Gentry," David said from the door.

"Matt," Jim said.

"Can you walk outside with me a minute, Jim?" Matt said. "I'd like you to look at Chester's front shoe."

"I can do that for you, sir," David said and wiped his hands, ready to untie the leather apron around his waist.

Matt shook his head, staring at Jim all the while. "That's all right, David. I'd like to speak to Jim. Alone."

Jim pulled his apron off, rolled down his sleeves, and followed Matt outside and around the back of the forge building. Chester was standing quietly chewing on some grass and nickered when he saw Matt.

"What's the matter with him?"

Matt turned to him. "With Chester? Nothing. Nothing at all."

"Then what is this about?" But he knew, he knew why Olivia's brother was staring at him, fists clenched, aching to take a swing.

"I think you know what this is about," Matt said, staring hard at him. "What happened between you and Livie at Harper's Ferry?"

"I don't know what you want me to say."

Matt shoved him hard, hard enough that his back hit the wall of the building with a thump.

"What in the goddamn hell happened between you and my sister?" he shouted.

David came around the side of the building and skidded to a stop.

"We're fine, David," Jim said. "Go back inside."

"Tell me, you son of a bitch!"

He couldn't betray her any more than he already had. "I have nothing to say to you."

Jim saw the fist coming. Knew it was going to be painful, and yet he didn't even raise his arms to cover his face. Matt was swinging hard and fast, and finally he pulled his forearms to his face, giving Matt a chance to pummel his stomach. He got hit hard in the kidneys and dropped to his knees.

"Defend yourself! Or can't you look me in the eye! I trusted you, and so did my mother!"

Jim was kneeling, hands on his thighs, watching the blood from his nose drip onto his pants. He had nothing to say to redeem himself.

"What are you doing, Matt?" he heard Adam say. "Get up, Jim."

"Do you realize what he did, Adam? Have you figured it out yet? This son of a bitch, my best friend, has . . . was with . . . oh, Christ, Livie," Matt said and walked away.

Adam Gentry knelt down. He handed Jim a handkerchief.

"I'm guessing since you were letting Matt swing freely, he's right. Otherwise, I'd sure as hell hope you'd take a swing back at him if he was talking casually about our sister's virtue."

Jim sat back against the side of the building and held the handkerchief under his nose. He could feel an eye swelling shut.

"I can't tell you how sorry I am," he said. "I've never had anything but the utmost respect for the Gentry family. I wish it hadn't happened, but it did."

"And she won't marry you?"

"Marry me? She's moving to Wash-ing-ton! There'll be lots of smart, eligible bachelors there to dote on her."

"Jim? You're going to want to be careful here. I'm not as big as you or Matt but I'm not afraid of you, either. If you're implying that Olivia is loose with her favors, I'm going to finish the job Matt started."

Jim turned his head sharply. "What do you mean by that?"

"I mean if you think what happened between the two of you meant so little to her that she'd merrily trip on to a new town and a new life and a new man, you know my sister much less well than I thought you did."

He could hear himself then. That's exactly what he'd said to her. That she'd be soon moving to Washington. "There will be someone to take my place when you're settled." Would she have thought that he thought she would lie with just anyone?

"Did she say no?" Adam asked.

"About what?"

Adam sat down beside him with a sigh and leaned against the wood slats. "When you asked her to marry you?"

Jim gulped. "I never asked her," he whispered.

"Well, good God, man," Adam said, shaking his head. "What in the almighty hell is the matter with you? Why not?"

"She's . . . she's special. She's perfect. She's Matt's sister, and yours, too. Matt and I had an agreement, even if neither of us had ever said it aloud. We'd never be free with each other's sisters. Anyway, she's meant to do great things."

"You're not young boys any longer! You're men. What a ridiculous notion!" Adam rubbed a hand down his face. "Look. You've got to fix this. You've made one hell of a mess." He stood up and reached down to help him stand.

His body hurt and he'd be more sore tomorrow. "I'm not sure what to do."

"Have you just tried talking to her?" Adam shook his head and held up a hand. "It's between the two of you, and I'll let you work it out the way you see fit, but," Adam said and stepped closer, tilting his head to look him in the eye, "if there are any consequences from what happened, you'll both be marching down the aisle faster than you can say I do. Got that straight?"

Jim nodded. Adam got on his horse and trotted out to the street where Matt was waiting. Emmaline came around the back of the forge carrying a tin bucket full of snow.

"Here," she said. "You're going to look a fool if you don't keep the swelling down. Why didn't you at least cover your face?"

The answer was obvious, finally. Physical pain was nothing. He could stand a great deal, he could endure most any test or challenge he faced. But talking? Talking to Livie? Telling her she meant everything to him, that his world started and ended with her? He was terrified. But he was going to have to find a way to do it.

CHAPTER 15

"I'm not hungry, Mother," Olivia said through her bedroom door. "I'm going to lie down."

"Shall I call for the doctor, Olivia?"

She blew out a breath. She supposed her mother was no longer going to allow her to hide in her rooms as she'd been doing over the past week.

"We've company for dinner, dear, and I would like you to join us."

Her mother used guilt persuasively even without meaning to. The Gentrys were entertaining, and Olivia's duty was to be present as part of it and gracious to guests of Paradise. If she'd heard that said once she'd heard it a thousand times. It was probably just Reverend Pendleton, and she'd not be required to say much.

"I'll be down in a moment."

She straightened her hair and dress and looked at herself in the mirror at her dressing table. She was tempted to dab some rouge on her cheeks, she looked so white and pasty, but she wasn't terribly concerned about her appearance lately. She'd feel better about herself when she moved to Washington, she told herself and attempted a smile. She looked ghastly if she were truthful. But there was nothing to come of it. She would get through this heartache and never allow herself to be hurt in such a way ever again.

Olivia opened the door to the dining room where dinner had already begun. "I'm so sorry to be late," she said as Adam, Matthew, and Jim Somerset stood. It took every bit of every single thing that made her a Gentry to keep her on her feet. She took a deep breath and walked to the chair on her mother's right.

Jim came around Adam's chair. He stood looking at her while she concentrated on the roses embroidered on the toes of her slippers. She sat in the chair he pulled out and looked at the plate in front of her.

"I've brought you some flowers," he said. "Your mother put them there, on the buffet."

"Aren't they just lovely, Olivia?" Eleanor asked.

"Wherever did you get them at this time of year, Jim?" Annie said.

"You're making me look bad, Somerset!" Matt said with too jolly a laugh.

Jenny was at her elbow. "Just some wine, please Jenny," she said. "And perhaps some soup."

She gulped her wine when it arrived and refused to look up. She'd never been so uncomfortable in her life. Everyone knew. Everyone at the table knew that she'd lain with him. She'd been naked with him and gloried in the feel of him, the weight of him, and how he felt when he was inside of her.

She'd made one trip to town two days after she'd come home, when Aunt Brigid insisted she needed a certain color embroidery thread and there was no one else to get it. She'd stood behind the shelves in the mercantile and heard Emmaline tell Marabelle that Jim's broken nose and blackened eye had been the result of a fight. They'd whispered Matt's name, but she'd heard.

She bought her thread from Marabelle, never meeting her

friend's eye, and went directly to Matt and Annie's home. Annie had told her after some significant prodding that, yes, Matt had suspected the worst and paid Jim a visit. Adam had, too. Her humiliation had been total and complete. She wanted to be away to a new home in Washington but found she didn't have the strength or motivation to begin the preparations for a house of her own. Aunt Brigid had said she was in a decline. It was true, and she had no earthly idea how to climb out of it or even to find the will to fight it.

She ate her soup and listened to the contrived conversation and the long uncomfortable silences. Coffee was finally served with one of her favorite desserts, bread pudding with caramel sauce. She took one bite and laid her spoon down.

"I think I'll retire," she said and stood.

"We were going to have a cordial in the main room, Livie. Won't you join us?" Adam asked.

She shook her head. "Good night everyone." She turned quickly to the door. She was suddenly panicked, breathing in short gasps, desperate to get away from them all, especially Jim Somerset, looking gorgeous and serious in his Sunday suit and tie, even if his eye was still yellow and bruised, and lock herself away in her rooms.

"I was hoping to have a chance to speak to you," Jim said after clearing his throat several times.

"I can't think of anything we would need to discuss."

"No. I don't imagine you can, but would you please accompany me on a short walk outside? I find I need some air."

And she knew she might as well go with him and listen to him and be humiliated all over again. It would be done then. Perhaps she needed some closure and needed to break free of all the manners and restraint that she'd been schooled to since she was a young girl. Perhaps she would let go of all things that held her back from saying what might cleanse her and allow her some peace to move on.

HE DIDN'T THINK SHE WAS GOING TO GO WITH HIM TO FIND some privacy, and his stomach was revolting from the leaden-tasting food and sour wine he'd just had and from nerves waiting for her answer. He couldn't remember a more tense, uncomfortable hour he'd ever spent in all of his life. He'd come and asked Mrs. Gentry the day before if he would be able to speak to Olivia. She'd come up with the plan for him to come to dinner the following day, and he'd readily complied. It was all he could do to look her in the eye, although Mrs. Gentry appeared to be her normal serene self.

His mother was still not speaking to him once she'd seen his face and asked who'd done that to him. Of course, Emmaline had shared the scene behind the forge and then left him there twisting in the wind as he stood in front of his mother in the sitting room. He'd watched her put two and two together and seen her face wash with horror and shame.

Jenny held Olivia's coat, and Olivia looked at it as if assessing something more far -reaching than a walk to the stone patio. Matt looked as if he wanted to break his nose again or maybe crack a rib or two.

Finally, she pushed her arms through the sleeves of her coat and turned and left the room. He heard the front door open.

"Go," Adam said to him and shooed him with his hand. "Go!"

Jim followed her outside to the drive where she stood staring up at the sky as it grew dark.

"I want to apologize, Olivia," he said. "I took terrible advantage of you, and of your family's trust."

He watched as her face changed from bewilderment to anger. Her fists clenched at her sides.

"How dare you? How dare you?" she bit out.

"I know. I should have never come in your room that day. You deserved so much more."

She stepped close to him. Her teeth were clenched and her eyes were filled with fire. "And that's what you have to say to me? That's why you think I'm angry? That's why you came here tonight? I would dearly love to slap you, but it appears my over-bearing brother Matthew has beaten me there."

"What do you want me to say?"

She shook her head and looked at him with such disappoint-ment and disillusionment that he took a step back from her. He didn't know what to do. He didn't know how to solve this tangle to both of their satisfactions.

"I'm in love with you, Jim. I've been in love with you all of my life," she said and took a deep breath, her voice rising. "I wanted you that night. I wanted to make love to you because there will never, ever be another man that I would want to be intimate with. You're it. You're the only one."

"I . . . I . . ."

"Don't. Don't cheapen how I feel with your declaration of trust to the Gentry family with no declaration for me!" she screamed as tears rolled down her cheeks. "This wasn't all about you and your precious honor, Jim Somerset!"

He would have fallen to his knees had a leaf landed on his shoulder he was so shocked. She loved him. She'd always loved him. And he would be the only man to ever touch her in the way that he'd done.

"I came here to ask you to marry me," he whispered.

"Did you? How unfortunate for you," she said. "I'm done being tossed around in love by you. I am done. Do you hear me? You told me years ago you'd never, ever marry me or love me, and I finally believe you."

He watched her go inside, leaving him staring at the house, now lit softly through the windows. The door opened again and for one moment his heart leapt with joy, but it wasn't Olivia. Just Matt bringing his coat.

"Here. Put this on and go home. I think Livie's done talking."

He nodded and went to the stables to retrieve his horse. He was leaving his mind and heart at Paradise.

* * *

OLIVIA WALKED IN THE HOUSE AND PAST HER FAMILY STILL sitting around the dining room table. She stopped herself and returned to the open doorway.

"Matthew. Do not ever, ever insert yourself into my business, or so help me God I'll not speak to you again."

Adam raised his brows, and Matt sputtered.

"Shush, Matt," Annie said. "You've done and said enough."

Her mother had a strange smile on her face. "Good night, darling. Let's plan some shopping tomorrow for your move to Washington."

"Yes, mother, I'd like that," she said. "Good night."

OLIVIA WOKE THE NEXT DAY FEELING AS IF A GREAT WEIGHT had lifted from her. Her heart was not mended—she didn't know if it ever would be—but the blanket of malaise that had hovered over her for weeks seemed to be gone. She'd said what needed said. She would move on. Jenny handed her a letter from Josephine at the noonday meal. She could hardly wait to get to her room and read it.

She read Josephine's reply to her letter aloud at the dinner table that evening.

Darien has found the perfect house for you. Only two streets away from me on an avenue with young families and some older people, too. It has been remodeled with all the newest conveniences, although there is no furniture at all. You would have to begin from scratch. Think about coming to town to see it yourself and decide if you would like to make an offer. Bring that brother of yours if you don't mind.

Olivia looked up and smiled, even knowing that with every

step she took she was putting distance between herself and her family, those she loved most in the world.

"Well, Adam? What do you think? Shall we go look at the house?" she asked.

"I'll go," Matt said. "I've not been as good a brother as I should have been. I'd like you to show me around so that I can see all the reasons you want to move there."

"Perhaps, Matt, you could do something else wonderful for Olivia. I'd like to escort her," Adam said.

Matt harrumphed a laugh. "I'm sure you would like to get another look at Darien's sister. Why can't we both go? Would you like to go, Annie? We could get a hotel room and go to those warehouses that mother told you about. It's time we had more furniture than a table in the kitchen and a bed."

"How exciting!" Annie said. "I've never been to a big city!"

Matt kissed her forehead and smiled. "Then we will go and make a honeymoon of it."

Eleanor lifted her wineglass. "To Olivia and her next adventure!"

* * *

"I haven't seen you for some time, Louise," Eleanor Gentry said as the two women seated themselves in the Somerset sitting room.

"You may set the coffee here, Helen," Louise said. She turned to pour and handed Eleanor a cup. "It's so pleasant to have a few temperate days during these cold months, is it not?"

"Oh, yes. I needed to be out and about and thought what a lovely day for a ride and a visit with an old friend."

Louise dropped her head, staring at her lap. "You are an old friend and I can't act as if there is nothing to be said, but I don't know what to say exactly."

Eleanor patted her hand. "Please don't fret. Whatever is

between Jim and Olivia must be worked out between the two of them. As much as they are still, and always will be our children, they are adults. I think they must work this out in their own way, if there is something to be worked out that is."

Jim stood near the sitting room door after Emmaline had told him she saw Mrs. Gentry ride up. He'd wiped his hands and hurried inside, sneaking down the hallway like a thief. He could hear every bit of the conversation, and he was sorry beyond words that his mother felt ashamed to speak to one of her oldest friends. Thank the dear Lord his father wasn't alive to see his son's downfall, but there was something heartbreaking about his mother's shame. He was going to carry that for a long while.

"Well, you are more forbearing than I. I still cannot quite believe it of my son, even knowing it's true."

"Don't waste years or days or even minutes being angry, Louise. Life is far too short. And I have no doubt that Olivia was party to it as well."

"How did dinner go? Emmaline told me you invited him. He rode the whole way to Middletown to a grower who raises hothouse flowers to bring a bouquet to Olivia."

"And they were beautiful. He looked very handsome, I will say that. They didn't speak over dinner, it *was* rather awkward, but they did step outside together for a few minutes."

"Perhaps there is some hope then for the two of them. It has always been so clear to me that he loved her."

"Yes. I do believe he does, and I'm certain she loves him. But the fact of the matter is that Olivia will be traveling to Washington to finalize the purchase of a home there very soon."

"Oh. Oh, dear," his mother said. "I heard she was considering it. What a bold move! I can't help but admire it, although I am fairly petrified for her, Eleanor. I'm just as afraid that my Jim will plod along doing the right thing and never grab his chance for happiness. He will do his duty and, I fear, little else."

Jim leaned back against the wall of the hallway. He would plod along and be pitied. He and Emmaline most likely. They would live together in this house when mother died and go to church together and ramble on about days long gone. Nieces and nephews and neighbors would say, "Oh yes. Jim and Emmaline Somerset still live together in the family homestead. No. Neither ever married."

He was awakened from that depressing daydream when the door to the sitting room opened.

"Oh, Jim. I didn't know you were in the house or I would have had you pay your respects to Mrs. Gentry."

"Ma'am," he said and nodded.

"Jim. How nice to see you," Eleanor said.

"Likewise, ma'am."

His mother linked arms with Mrs. Gentry, and she called to Phillip to get their guest's horse. He stood there watching them and thinking about what they'd said. His mother turned back to him, and he followed her into the sitting room once Mrs. Gentry was gone. She sat down in her usual chair by the fire and picked up her coffee cup.

"Mrs. Gentry has been imploring me to let go of my anger toward you. It's a miracle the woman will step over the threshold of this house considering all that has happened."

"I'm as sorry today as I was yesterday. I'm not sure there is anything left for me to do other than hope I am once again in your good graces."

She looked up sharply. "Nothing to do? There is nothing for you to do?" she said shrilly. "Perhaps you should shed this mantle of propriety and find some passion in your life! Your father and I were passionate for each other. No. Don't turn away from me. You will hear me out! We were never showy or ridiculous about our love but that did not diminish it, not one bit. You will live the rest of your life, it seems, in some quiet penance, for what I don't know. But . . . I loved your father." Her eyes welled with tears. "I miss him desperately in my everyday life, in the lives of our children, and in—" She stopped, dabbed her eyes with the twisted hanky in her hand and looked up at him red-faced. "And in our intimate lives. Our private world where the two of us could be as passionate and demonstrative as we wished. I would have married him a hundred times even knowing our time together would be cut short and knowing the sorrow and ache I would feel for him. Don't be a fool, James. Please, don't be a fool."

He watched his mother leave the room, head high, as if she hadn't just referred to something that was horribly embarrassing for her to say and for him to hear. But he'd heard it, and it was a truth all the same. Was that what was missing from his life? Had the weight of his responsibilities crushed any passions he might have had? Was it possible to resurrect them?

He saddled his horse and went for a long ride. Perhaps he would take a long ride the next day and the next day, too, until he puzzled out or gathered the courage to tell Livie how he felt. He had quite a bit of thinking to do. Or maybe he should stop thinking and start doing. Maybe that's what he needed to think about.

* * *

ELEANOR AND OLIVIA AND AUNT BRIGID HAD SPENT A QUIET morning later that week looking through catalogs of furniture and wall coverings. Matt, Annie, Adam, and she would travel together on the following Saturday to see this town house and perhaps even make an offer on it. She'd not yet completed her letter to Josephine asking her or Darien to make arrangements for a suite of rooms for Matt and Annie at a hotel near her home. Teddy was staying with Mother and Aunt Brigid, and both were excited at the prospect of having him all to themselves.

Olivia sat at her dressing table, looking at herself in the mirror, then letting her eyes blur until she could picture him staring at her that night. Asking her to marry him. She would relive those few moments again and again it seemed. She blew out a breath and pinched her cheeks. She had laughed today at some random and hilarious comment that Aunt Brigid had made. It was the first time she'd done so in weeks, if memory served her, and she wasn't the only one to notice. Her mother stared at her, smiling for a long moment even after they'd continued looking at davenport fabrics.

Adam seated her at the dining room table just as Matt and Annie came in carrying Teddy.

"I didn't know you were joining us," Eleanor said and rose. "Jenny, please set two more places and see if Beatrice is able to watch Teddy for a few minutes."

"I don't want to put anyone to trouble," Annie said. "I made curtains for Teddy's room and didn't get anything ready for lunch. Matt said . . ."

"Don't worry a moment, dear," Eleanor said. "There is always plenty, and Mabel revels in having you both here to fuss over. Tell me which fabric you chose finally. The blue or the white?"

This was what she would miss the most, Olivia thought. The normal everyday living. The regular meals and details of one's lives and children's lives that could only be gained in some proximity. It would be very hard to learn to eat alone. They joined hands as Adam said grace and had just begun passing platters when the double doors to the dining room slammed opened with a bang, rattling their glass panes.

Jim Somerset stood there, bringing cold air with him.

CHAPTER 16

"I've been out riding all morning."

Olivia looked up at him from under fringed lashes as she sat at the dining room table with her family. Staring at him with those heavenly green eyes.

"Are you staying for luncheon, Mr. Somerset?" Jenny asked.

He shook his head, his eyes never leaving Olivia's face. He swallowed, desperate to remember all the things he'd promised himself to say to her as he rode through the woods and let Jasper have his head on the trails over the last few hours. But maybe he'd better just begin.

"I love you. I love you so much I can't breathe sometimes. I have loved you since the very first time you showed me an arrowhead you'd found out at the cave by the old springhouse. I didn't know what it meant then to love you, and I've been a fool for years watching as you nearly slipped away, but I know now. I don't want you to go anywhere without me. I'm in love with you."

She stood slowly and faced him. Tears were brimming in her eyes and her bottom lip was quivering. "You never told me," she whispered. "Even when—"

He shook his head. "I didn't. I was a fool. All I know is what I know now. I love you, Olivia Gentry. I want to marry you. I can't bear the thought of living this life without you."

She blinked, and a lone tear trailed down her cheek. He wiped it away with his thumb.

"I'll hire a manager for the forge until Phillip is able to work it himself. If I need to learn another trade in Washington or wherever you want to live, I'll learn it. Just give me a chance."

Her lips were trembling and her chest was rising and falling in time with each breath she took. He took two steps forward and gathered her in his arms, lifting her against him until they were eye to eye, her feet dangling against his shins. He kissed her, holding the back of her head, and touching the seam of her lips with his tongue. She put her palms on his cheeks and slid her hands slowly into his hair. He heard someone clear their throat, and he walked backward until they were in the hallway.

"I love you, Livie."

She was crying too hard to speak. She kissed his eyes and his cheeks and his mouth.

"Come away with me now. We'll go to Middletown where there's a hotel. I'll find someone to marry us. Right now. I love you, and I've wasted too much time."

"Wait here. Will you?" she asked.

He nodded. "This is the moment I've been waiting for, after all. I'll wait forever."

He stood in the hallway and took a quick look into the Gentry dining room through the paned glass door. Matt was glaring at him, and his wife was crying. Adam was laughing, and Mrs. Gentry was slicing something on her plate as if she didn't have a care or worry in the world. Aunt Brigid winked at him, and he smiled at her. Olivia hurried back down the hallway from the stairs, carrying a small leather satchel. Her gloves were on and she'd pulled on a long coat and riding boots.

She looked at him. "You're certain, Jim? This is not guilt

driving you to do this? I love you desperately, but I'll not force your hand. I love you too much for that."

He put a finger under chin and tilted her head up to look at him. "Real and abiding love and passion like mine are not prompted by guilt. I believe there is a grand passion between us and our love will only deepen as we get older. Marry me, Livie. I love you."

She turned away and opened the door to the dining room. "Mother," she said. "I'm going with Jim."

"How lovely, dear," Eleanor said and looked at Jim with a smile. "Do be careful with Olivia, Jim. She's precious to us."

SHE RODE JASPER TO MIDDLETOWN WHILE HE RODE YORK. SHE wanted him to ride the big stallion that he'd ridden to rescue her at Harper's Ferry. She wanted him to ride the horse her father had loved so much. The same horse that had gotten Daddy home after he'd been shot. It was silly, but she couldn't help herself. She wanted her father's horse with her when she married Jim Somerset.

It had taken two hours on good roads, fortunately with no rain, to get to Middletown. He'd gone directly to the hotel, a rather large and lovely one for a smaller town, and reserved a room for them. She waited there while he went to speak to the preacher and lay down on the bed but didn't not fall asleep. Jim came back in the room, and when he saw her stretched out, he growled.

"Come on, Livie," he said. "The minister is going to marry us."

She stood and straightened her hair. She had changed into a pale yellow dress she'd always loved. "Did you have any trouble convincing him?"

Jim harrumphed. "Well, it seems your brothers, Phillip, and I are going to put a new roof on the parsonage sometime this spring."

She laughed. "You needn't go to that trouble. We can wait until tomorrow."

"No, we can't. We're getting married in the next hour, and then we're going to sleep together as man and wife. Right there in that bed."

She felt the heat of a blush rise from her neck to her face. "Then we'd best not be late."

* * *

SHE STARED AT THE WEDDING RING HE'D SLIPPED ON HER finger. She was married to Jim Somerset. All of her girlish dreams had come true. She looked up at him as they walked back to the hotel, hand in hand. He was smiling and nodding as people passed, and tipping his hat to the ladies. He was hers, she thought, suddenly. He was hers alone and she was his.

"I've asked to have our meal delivered to our room," he said. "I'm hungry as a bear, and I interrupted your noonday meal. I'm going to the bathhouse for men on the first floor of the hotel, and I've asked to have a bath sent up for you. By the time we're both done, dinner will be ready for us."

"You've thought of everything," she said.

He smiled and kissed her hand. "I've been imagining this day for a long time."

Olivia bathed and hummed a tune as she did. She was a married lady. She dried and pulled on a green satin nightgown she'd had made the last time she and Mother were in Philadelphia. It hung from thin straps to the floor with lace edging the neckline and the hem of the robe. How happy she was she'd remembered that she had it and thrown it in her satchel at the last minute.

"Livie?"

She opened the door. He'd shaved his beard and mustache completely off and was more devastatingly handsome than she thought it possible for him to be. He was staring at her now and licked his lips. He stepped in the room as the hotel staff wheeled a cart with plates covered with metal lids and a bottle of something chilling in a bucket of ice to the door.

JIM PULLED THE CART INSIDE THEIR ROOM. HE POURED THEM both a glass of champagne, drank his in one swallow and tipped the waiter. He'd already told the man he didn't want them disturbed until morning. He turned and looked at her. At his bride. She was as lovely as he'd ever seen her.

"You're so very beautiful," he whispered. "So perfect."

She shook her head and unbuttoned the robe she wore over a silky gown. She shrugged her shoulders and let it fall to the floor. "I'm not perfect," she said. "If I were perfect, I could control myself. But I can't. I want to touch you."

He pulled his shirt over his head and sat down on the edge of the bed to pull off his boots never taking his eyes from hers. He unbuttoned his pants, took them off, and stood in front of her in just his flannel knee-length drawers. She looked at him slowly, up and down. He bent down on his haunches and picked up the hem of her gown and looked up at her for permission. She was breathing heavily and her eyes were dreamy. She nodded. He stood, pulling the gown over her head as he did.

He palmed her breasts, and she fluttered a long sigh as if she'd been waiting forever for him to touch her. Her nipples hardened against his hand. "Lie down," he whispered. "I want to taste you everywhere."

Her eyes widened as she lay back against the pillows and he pulled off his drawers. He was as erect as it was possible to be. She stared at his cock and then looked up at him from under her lashes. She licked her lips and touched him there lightly with her fingers, finally wrapping her hand about him and running her thumb over the tip. He moaned, barely able to drag his eyes away from her hand as it moved up and down, up and down.

He broke her hold on him, stretching out beside her, kissing her openmouthed, moving his tongue in and out of hers, tracing her lips. He moved down her body, running his tongue over her nipples until she groaned, and licking one and flicking the other with his thumb. She arched off the bed and cried out as he held her full breast in his hand and sucked hard on the nipple.

"I love you, Livie. I'll love you forever."

He kissed her stomach and lower still, her eyes on him as he kissed her inner thigh and spread her legs wide. He could not stop staring at her there.

"Jim. I can't . . . I don't . . ."

He knelt between her legs and touched his tongue to her then. She jerked and he held her hips still while he prodded her with his fingers and licked her and found the spot that made her writhe against him, pulling at his hair, until she threw her arms above her head and stilled. The look on her face was wholly erotic, her cheeks flushed, her mouth parted as she touched her tongue to her top lip, threatening to make him spend before he could satisfy them both at the same time.

"Jim," she whispered. "Jim. Please."

He climbed above her, positioned her hips, and thrust into her. He worked himself slowly back and forth until she opened her eyes and reached up to pull his face down to kiss him openmouthed. She was wet and warm and tight around his cock and lay passive beneath him until she began to move again, her eyes fluttering half open and then closing.

"Come with me, Livie," he said and strained. She arched off the bed, and he threw his head back, letting himself plant inside of her at the deepest point. He shuddered and dropped onto her, her arms around his neck.

He was far too heavy to laze around on his wife even if it felt as though every bone in his body had turned to jelly. He rolled on his back, pulled her with him, and kissed her head and mouth.

"I love you, Olivia Somerset. There's babies in our future," he whispered.

"There are. I love you, husband," she said and smiled up at him dreamily. Her eyes opened wide then and she looked up at him. "Where did you ever learn about . . . about putting your . . . you know . . . there," she asked, her face suddenly flaming red.

He smiled at her and rolled her onto her back. "There's books, Livie. Lots of them. The Romans wrote them."

She smiled back at him. "Then we must make a study of them. Together."

"Yes," he said. "And we have a lifetime to do it."

EPILOGUE

"Mother! Aunt Brigid!" Olivia called as she went through the front door at Paradise. "The newlyweds are home!"

The dining room doors opened wide and she was surrounded by her family, her mother hugging her to her, swaying and holding her tightly. Eleanor whispered in her ear, "Oh, how I wish your father could see you, but I imagine he can. It's just that I wish he were here with you now."

"I wish he were here, too. We took York to Middletown. It made me feel as if Daddy were there."

"Of course, it did," Eleanor said and kissed her forehead.

Matt grabbed her and swung her around, and she kissed Annie, who was crying and squeezing her hands.

"You are the picture of happiness, Livie," she said. "I'm so happy for you!"

She walked into Adam's arms as he held them open to her. They came around her tightly. He kissed the top of her head and shushed her when she gulped down tears.

"You've made the perfect choice, sweetheart. You never lost sight of yourself, but in the end love has won out, has it not?"

She nodded against his chest. "It has. I love him, Adam."

"I know you do," he said and set his chin on top of her head.

She could see Aunt Brigid making Jim bend over and kiss her cheek, and then Jenny and Mabel kissed him, too, and fussed over him as well. Matt was slapping his back, and Adam released her to shake his hand and pull him into a hug. Jenny opened the door when someone knocked.

Louise Somerset and all of her children, and grandchildren, too, came through the entryway, explaining that she'd received Jim's telegram about their planned arrival back in Winchester and that she couldn't wait one second longer to see them. Louise came straight to Olivia and hugged her and kissed her, dabbing at her eyes. "I couldn't be any happier for you or for my son. You are glowing, Olivia," she said and kissed her cheeks. "Just glowing with love and happiness."

"There's bridal cake and coffee," Jenny said as she helped the Somersets off with their wraps and shepherded them into the main room.

"A bridal cake?" Olivia said. "But you didn't know when we would return."

Eleanor laughed. "Mabel's been baking one every morning, just in case. She gives Matthew the one from the day before."

Matt rubbed his stomach and blew out a breath. "It's about time you got home. They want me to eat a cake every morning. I just got done eating yesterday's."

Jim stood behind her, and she looked up at him over her shoulder. He mouthed "I love you," and she smiled up at him with all the love and passion she felt for him. She was reminded how very fortunate she was to be part of such a large and loving family.

Everyone seated themselves as the cake was served, and Adam cleared his throat. "I think the bride may have something to say."

"I do," Olivia said to all those near and dear to her now looking up at her. "I'm hoping Mother and Aunt Brigid do not mind if my husband," she said and blushed and looked at him, as the men shouted and the women sighed, "and I live here at

Paradise until we can build a home somewhere here in Winchester. We'll not be moving to Washington."

Louise Somerset began to cry again. Eleanor was looking at Olivia, her hands together under her chin. Jim's sisters clapped.

"That doesn't mean we won't be visiting other cities and maybe even far-off places. But we want to live here, in Winchester, close to our families," Jim said and looked down at her, his love and devotion shining in his eyes. "My wife is special, very special, and she's meant for great things. I can't wait to see what they are."

AUTHOR NOTES

Thank you for purchasing *For This Moment*, the third installment in the Gentrys of Paradise series. I hope you enjoyed it. The novella, *Into the Evermore,* is the first book of the series and tells the story of Eleanor and Beauregard Gentry's meeting and marriage. The next book, *For the Brave*, is Matt Gentry's story and how Annie Campbell saved him from a spring flooded river and his own demons. The final book in the series is Adam Gentry's story, *For Her Honor.* It will release in the fall of 2018.

The Crawford Family series remains popular and includes, *Train Station Bride, Contract to Wed, The Maid's Quarters*, and *Her Safe Harbor*. This series details the lives of three wealthy Boston-born sisters. *Romancing Olive* chronicles the life of a sheltered Philadelphia spinster as she heads west to save a niece and nephew. *Reconstructing Jackson* is the story of Reed Jackson, crippled confederate officer, who moves west to begin again, post-Civil War. *Cross the Ocean* and *Charming the Duke* are two British Victorian-era romances.

If you enjoyed *For This Moment*, please post a review or share your thoughts with friends and family. News about my books is available at my website, hollybushbooks.com. I post regularly on my FaceBook page with excerpts from all my books and I welcome you to join my FaceBook Group, Holly's Heroines. Thank you again for your purchase!

The first few pages of *Train Station Bride* are next! Enjoy!

Boston 1887

"Really, Julia, do hurry," Jane Crawford said to her daughter, who was still seated at the ivory lace-covered vanity. "The guests are arriving, and you should be there to greet them."

Julia Crawford smiled up at her mother with resignation. This was a battle she didn't need to win. She would make no argument.

"I'll be down shortly, Mother. Jolene and Jennifer are there. Our guests are here to see them, not me. Has Jillian gone down?"

"She is standing with your father at the door," her mother replied.

"I'll be down in a moment, then. Do go down to the guests. You know how father fusses when you leave him alone," Julia said as she spun a blond curl around her finger.

Jane glided to the door and closed it softly. Julia cocked her head, waiting for the soft patter of her mother's slippers on the steps. Only then did she pull the gold chain from her neck and insert the key that hung from it into a gilded jewel box. With a final glance at the door, she pulled a white envelope from the box and removed and unfolded the letter it held.

Dear Miss Crawford,

I will be at the train station to meet you on the appointed day. My mother and I look forward to your arrival. I will stay above my shop until the day of our marriage. My mother has graciously allowed you to stay with her during that time. She is pleased to know you do needlepoint.

Her arthritic hands no longer allow her to sew, and she is most anxious to have another woman about. I am anxious as well . . .

Julia read to the last line even though she could have recited the letter as if it were the Lord's Prayer. *Very truly, Mr. Jacob Snelling.* The day of her departure would arrive sooner than she both hoped and dreaded. Mr. Snelling was a successful shop owner in a small South Dakota town, near fifty years old, with an aging mother. He had never married. His mother had begun to complain of a lack of company, and he admitted he was lonely. Those two forces had led him to place an ad for a wife in the *Boston Globe* nearly a year ago. To Julia's shock, she had answered it. Their correspondence had been proper, more formal than she'd expected from a merchant in the Midwest.

That formality had been a great comfort to her—it was what she was accustomed to. He sounded like a truly nice man. He had great regard for his mother, of that she was certain. His letters were filled with news of the aging Portentia Snelling, and that always calmed Julia when she was most terrified of what she was embarking on. A man so devoted to his own mother would certainly be kind to her. She rose from the vanity seat with a smile on her face. One more formal evening with her family could not deter her.

Julia greeted a few guests and then found an unoccupied chair in a corner of the library. She had spent much of the day arranging the fresh flowers that now filled the room. It had kept her mind and hands occupied while her sisters fussed over their wardrobe and their mother scolded the servants over some small matter. Without distractions, the day would have dragged on, and she would have dwelled on a decision her mind had yet to grasp fully. She gazed absently about the room.

Her older sister, Jolene, married now ten years with a beautiful, fair child, sashayed about on the arm of her husband, Turner

Crenshaw. Julia's younger sister, Jennifer, nearly twenty-one, sat amidst a bevy of Boston's first sons, laughing sweetly and tilting her head just so. It was most certainly the sin of envy that would lead Julia straight to Hades in the afterlife.

She felt no jealousy, though, as her eyes found Jillian. Dressed in navy velvet with a cream-colored lace collar to match her hair, Jillian was the fairest of the Crawford family. The baby of the family at only ten years old, she was already beautiful enough to turn male heads. She'd spend the first hour of the party with the adults and then be whisked away to her rooms. Even at her young age she was a model of deportment and graciousness, with a gay laugh. Julia would miss her most of all.

The Crawford women were all tall and slender—except Julia. She'd been no higher than her father's tiepin at fourteen and still exactly the same height at twenty-seven. She snatched three shrimps from the young serving girl's tray as she passed and laid them beside four chocolate bonbons in the napkin on her lap. Julia preferred to refer to herself as pleasingly plump or, on the days before her monthly courses, as a fat, frothy, ugly spinster with perfectly beautiful siblings and parents.

She was licking chocolate from her fingers when she saw her mother staring. Jane Crawford excused herself from her guests gracefully, as she did everything in life, Julia had long ago decided. Gracefully floating, serene and above the clutter and clamor of normal living. She had attempted to instill that elegance in each of her children. Julia was certain her mother considered her second daughter her greatest failure.

"Julia, use a napkin," Jane chided and turned her head to view the crowd in their formal sitting room. "Alred McClintok has been hoping to speak to you all evening. Why don't you quit hiding in this corner and go talk to him?"

Julia dabbed chocolate from the corner of her mouth and looked at the man her mother was referring to. Did everyone assume that plump women were only attracted to fat men? One of the reasons Julia had continued writing Mr. Snelling was his description of himself in an early letter: *I am of medium height and very thin. Dear Mama worries I am ill, but Dr. Hammish assures me* . . . Alred McClintok was busy stuffing canapés in his mouth, leaving a trail of grease around his fleshy red lips. He reminded Julia of a large black ball propped on two very stubby sticks.

"I'm perfectly happy here, Mother. Your party seems a rousing success." Changing subjects had been a tactic Julia had used successfully when conversation turned in her direction, especially with her father and Jennifer. Her mother and Jolene, however, rarely allowed such a diversion unless it was to their advantage.

Julia knew she had failed when her mother gave her a glare she was long accustomed to. The icy blue of her mother's eyes and the pinched shell of her mouth screamed "spinster," "on the shelf," and a long list of other shortcomings without saying a word.

"Mr. McClintok is a customer of your father's, dear. We must always endeavor to make your father's bank prosperous. House-hold expenses only seem to rise, rather than fall," her mother said.

The veiled reference to Julia's dependence on her parents' home did not escape her. She also knew the Crawford Bank was very successful. Feeding and clothing her would never send them to the poorhouse. Julia glanced at the shrimp still lying in the napkin on her lap. Maybe she'd best go speak to the man. Nothing would come of a quick introduction, and it might keep her from expanding her waistline yet another inch. If he spat lamb on her gown, she could go to her rooms to change and not emerge until morning. Or she could slip away via the servants' staircase in the kitchen and check her bags, which were already packed and stacked in her dressing room. On the morrow there would be only three days until she departed.

Julia had hoarded every bit of silver she could for her trip. The letter to her family was written, as well as a separate one for Jillian. Their housekeeper, Eustace, would give them out when she didn't arrive home from a purported weeklong visit with Aunt

Mildred. By that time she would be married, and there would be nothing her family could do.

Jolene would roll her eyes. Jennifer would be sad—not for long, though. Her father would rant and rave. Her mother's fury would be hidden behind a glassy stare. Though, all in all, Julia was sure they would be glad she was gone. They would never voice the sentiment, for certain. It would be gauche to admit this final lapse in her judgment would, thankfully, be the last, in their company at least. They would tell friends she was on an extended holiday at Aunt Mildred's, just as they had done before. Soon no one would inquire as to when she would be coming home. Her family least of all.

The only person other than Eustace who would miss her would be Jillian. No more long walks in the park. No more reading together by candlelight with the rest of the household long abed. No more brushing the silken hair 'til the child's eyes drooped. Jane Crawford supposed Jillian preferred Julia's company because Julia often acted with the sense of a ten-year-old rather than that of a woman. Julia would insist that Jillian loved the freedom to just be herself in Julia's company. For whichever reason, they would miss each other desperately.

But it was long past time that Julia did something for herself. Made something of herself, even if it was only a wife to a thin, balding Midwesterner and a companion for his mother. She could have lived indefinitely with Aunt Mildred. Her aunt had written her as much. Julia loved her, and her aunt adored her, but Mildred at seventy-two had an active life with other widows in the seaside town she lived in. And a beau in his eighty-fourth year. As Mrs. Jacob Snelling, Julia would be someone of her own making. Someone's wife. Something no one could take away from her.